THE RAVEN GIRL

A novel by

KATHY CECALA

This is a work of fiction. Names, characters, places and events are used fictitiously. Any resemblance to actual events, locales, persons living or dead, is entirely coincidental.

ISBN#: 978-1461066378
Printed in the United States of America

Cover photo taken by the author
Cover design by Frank Cecala

1.

Colm, the priest's boy, scampered along the stony, fog-clogged shore of Inis Ghall, making his way toward the pagan caves. Early March was still winter in this part of Ireland, and a hint of snow lingered in the dawn air. The boy danced close to the edge of the waves, jumping away when the icy surf threatened to bite his bare toes. He kept his eyes cast down as he made he way toward the forbidden side of the island, oblivious to the cold, dressed only in a shirt of coarse, tattered wool which covered him from shoulder to knees.

He was searching for treasure. Above, flocks of gulls and terns shrieked, swirling and gliding in and out of the fog. But the mists were beginning to rise, gradually revealing the beach ahead. Colm surveyed the wrack-strewn strand, fresh from last night's storm, and knew he'd find something. Now that ships out of Galway city were making for Iceland and the Norse isles on a regular basis, trading in cods and furs, there was always a chance of a shipwreck. Strange things had been washing up on the isle of Ghall for some time now: Wooden wine kegs and scraps of exotic cloth, waterlogged books and sometimes, bizarre huge nuts or seedpods his father said came from the Tropics, nuts the size of a man's head. Once, Colm saw something winking up at him in the sand, a circle of stamped silver, which fit neatly in his palm. It disappeared into his father's pocket, as soon as Colm showed it to him.

Colm combed the shore several times a day, or whenever he could escape his parents' attention. His mother was forever putting him to work at something boring, sorting greasy sheep's wool or pulling lice from his little sister's head. But along the shoreline, he had competition: Anhin, an old fisherman's wife, who scoured the surf while her mate trawled the strait for eels. She was an ancient cranky crone of perhaps sixty years, bent over with age but possessing a younger woman's quick, sharp temper.

Colm had trouble hiding from her, despite his small size. His hair, a fiery shade of red-gold, betrayed him like a beacon, even from a great distance. If she spotted him picking at the wrack ahead of her, she would come screaming down the beach at him, cursing and calling him names. "Child of sin!" she would spit at him, because he was the priest's son, and priests of the Church were not supposed to have wives or children. "Get off my strand!" she'd howl, although the strand belonged to no one on the isle, but to the mainland O hEynne.

It was a good morning: He had not yet encountered Anhin, nor did he see the telltale trudge marks of her cart in the wet sand.

He had not gone far when, in the midst of the fog, a distant shape and color caught his eye, something mingled, ensnared in the beached seaweeds. Something large, as big as porpoise perhaps. But he knew exactly what it was.

Corpses often washed ashore, almost always male, usually unlucky fishermen lost in a gale. He did not avoid them, because he was not afraid of the dead. And he knew the dead, though unpleasant to look upon, often had things of value to offer. He would not hesitant to pull off leather boots off a dead sailor or go through his pockets. His family was so desperately poor that anything the sea threw up on shore could only be a special prize, a gift from God to be eagerly accepted.

So he ventured closer to this new corpse, with some hope and anticipation. He was startled to see a tangle of inky black hair, and the pale linen of a city woman's shift.

A lass? He blinked in surprise. Women and girls did not generally go off to sea. It was considered bad luck by island fishermen to have a female in a boat. Colm tiptoed closer to her, gazing with no small amount of curiosity at this unexpectedly female creature.

The girl lay on the sand just above the surf, looking as if she had been dropped from the sky. Her dark mane twisted about her body, her hair coal-black and shiny as a raven's. Her face appeared rather serene, as if she were deep into a long, peaceful slumber. There was no wound, no sign of struggle or violence. She was a very young woman, and Colm could not guess her age.

3

Perhaps she was fifteen, sixteen years, younger than his mother.

What truly intrigued him was the girl's coloring and features. He had never seen another human being like her: So dark, her skin tawny and golden, like an oatcake left to brown on the griddle. Her face was broad, flat, with full lips and a small wide nose, cheekbones so high Colm thought she must be deformed. He felt a wave of sorrow for her, dying so young and in such an unpleasant way. Drowning, he thought, must be the worst sort of death, choking on brine then sinking to the depths of the ice-cold sea, only to be eaten by the fish.

But the fish had not touched this dark maiden. Colm, naturally curious, moved closer to her. Was she like the island maidens in all ways? he wondered, tempted to lift her shift. He saw there was something about her neck, a fiber cord with an ornament: A small orb, a dull gleam in the fog-shrouded light of dawn. He reached out to touch this shining pebble, round as a small bird's egg or berry, but darted back suddenly in shock. Beneath his fingers, the girl's skin was warm to the touch, not clammy cold as it should have been.

She was alive!

Colm then heard from behind him the guttural mutterings of Anhin, coming up the shore. Instead of running away, he stood his ground, waiting until she came into view. As soon as she saw him, his shock of orange hair, she began to shout as usual and wave her fist. She approached, but stopped short when she saw the dark maiden, sprawled on the sand beside him.

"What…what manner of lass is this?" Her eyes widened.

"I just came upon her myself, old woman. The waves tossed her up. But she still lives!"

Anhin edged closer to the girl.

"This is a bad thing, an evil omen." To Colm: "Boy, drag her back into the sea, before anyone else sees her."

"No! She's alive, t'would be murder!"

"Aaaaaaah!" Anhin spat into the sand. "Is that what your sinning father is preaching these days? Don't you know *what* this girl is?"

"No…."

Anhin leaned close to him, whispering fiercely. "She's a sorceress, a witch, sent to us from the Almighty, a sign of worse to come. She's a punishment, for our sins."

"What? Why? What have we done?"

"Ask your own lecherous father, begetting bastards when he should be pure. She's an omen, to be sure."

"Mam told me a story of maidens who live in the sea. Sometimes they have tails like fish. Or they are girls during the day, but seals at night. If you marry one, you can never be unfaithful to her, mam says. This girl…she must be one of them!"

"This girl is no selkie, no seal who swims in the sea—those are good creatures. This one is evil. 'Tis more likely she's a *murúch*, a mermaid. They are wicked things, who set out to lure the fishermen to their deaths."

"Look at the ornament she wears!"

Anhin now studied the little orb nestled in the hollow of the girl's neck.

"'Tis a pearl," she mumbled. "I've seen pearls that came from the mussel-shells of Lough Corrib. But this one…is quite fair. Quite fair." She went to reach for it with her bony fingers, but Colm caught her by the wrist, then ducked, as she moved to swat him.

"Don't steal!" he cried. "It's a Commandment!"

The girl stirred, murmuring something.

"She's coming to!"

"I *told* you to drag her back into the sea. No telling what she'll do, now that she's on land."

He glanced upshore. "We could take her to the pagan cave at the western point. No one goes there. Leave food for her. Perhaps she'll recover, and swim off again. Leave us alone."

"I'm not letting her swim off with that pearl. That'll fetch a fortune in Galway, on the Lombards' street." She pushed Colm up the beach. "There's my cart there. Get it and help me load her in."

Anhin took the girl's shoulders, while Colm grabbed her feet. They were smooth and surprisingly warm in his hands; he examined them briefly for signs of fishy scales or barnacles, but they seemed completely human, and well-shaped.

His eyes darted back to the girl's neck, the ornament on the string. The size and shape of a misshapen hazelnut, it now gleamed with an unearthly glow.

What if the girl *were* bewitched, an actual murúch? Colm's father, an educated man schooled in Galway city, sternly taught that there were no such things as witches or sprites or mermaids, only God and His Trinity; but his mother, who'd lived her whole life on the island, continued to whisper her fantastic tales into his ear at night, of men and women who turned into seals or eels or porpoises, of tiny elves who would wander the land and suck the very breath out of sleeping babes. Hadn't she told him once, too, of vindictive women who transformed themselves into black ravens, so they could perch on the shoulders of their enemies, and lead them into danger?

Maybe this girl was kin to those ravens. Her hair had the same black sheen that ravens' feathers had, and her skin was so dark.

He did not know what to think of her, but he sensed the fact of her existence had to be kept secret, for now. There was no telling how the other islanders might react to seeing her. Like Anhin, they might conclude she was a bad spirit and would want to kill her, but he wanted the girl to live. He was already becoming somewhat attached to her, pleased by her unusually dark but handsome face, the warm golden-brown of her skin.

As they trundled the girl toward the barren rocky west end of the island, pulling the squeaking, grunting cart through the sand, Anhin kept muttering about the pearl.

"Do not tell you father nor your mother of this," she snapped at Colm. "Tell no one, I swear, or I will come and rip out your miserable tongue."

The boy shook his head fiercely. "I won't."

7

"Because that pearl is mine. No one else will have it. I won't take it now. T'would be bad luck. But when she dies in that cave, I will come to claim it."

"She may not die."

"She will, because she has taken in too much of the sea. She has a fever and now the shaking. She'll have no use for that ornament."

They approached the great cliff, the place Colm's father said was forbidden to all island Christians, the cave where the pagans of old, sinful times were said to have conducted their godless services, murdering their captives. Human bones had been found within. Now, only the seabirds lived here by the thousands, puffins, petrels and terns squawking with great unholy noise above. There were several caves at various heights overlooking the sea, the largest just under the summit. Colm, who had been here many times in defiance of his father's warnings, scampered inside the lowest cave without fear. He cleared a space on the rock floor for the girl, and somehow he and Anhin managed to pull her inside, though he himself, a short boy, could barely stand up in the dark, dank cave.

Anhin pointed a crooked finger at him. "Don't touch my pearl. If I see it gone, I'll come after you, I will."

He nodded solemnly. Sometimes he thought Anhin herself was some kind of evil spirit or witch. How could she care more about a mere shiny stone than a living, breathing person made by God? It was impossible to understand some adults.

He waited until the old woman left, she and her cart some distance from the cave, before sitting down beside the shivering, shaking lass. He stared down at her. A stain of pink had spread across her bronzed cheeks, her lips frantically moving but no sound emerging. He rubbed a frond of cool, moist sea-grass across her blazing face. This seemed to calm her a bit. He would come later and bring hay, water, some scraps of his family's own meager fare, cooked roots and mutton gristle, whatever he could steal from his mother's hearth.

But he left her with a troubled heart. Had they done the right thing in saving her? Was she a good creature, or a malevolent one? Would she bring good fortune to Inis Ghall—a miserably poor isle that surely needed it—or untold sorrow and blackness? Only time would tell, and for now, he could do naught but return to his own home, and wait.

2.

In the city of Galway, the young scholar Aedan leaned over an ancient parchment, eagerly taking in the spidery text of a story he now knew by heart: the tale of the great Saint Brendan, the holy man who centuries before had sailed his skin boat west into the unknown world. Each time Aedan read this tale, he was dazzled by the descriptions of strange lands and seas to the west of Eire, with monsters and columns of crystal, island-forges belching smoke and fire.

As a young religious scholar, in training for the priesthood, he knew an avid interest in such things was unseemly. He should be, his teachers told him, more concerned with life in the next world, in Heaven alongside the Lord and his angels, than in any novelty that might exist on this earth. But he couldn't help himself.

Barely eighteen, Aedan was consumed with a burning, insatiable curiosity about the outside world that he tried to keep secret. Lord Fulke, the aristocratic priest and vicar of St. Alban's—who also served as his mentor—reminded him constantly that he had no real time for this "nonsense." He warned Aedan that he should be more concerned with the countless other things he needed to know and learn, if he were to become a priest. He needed to improve his Latin, Greek and Hebrew, and he had many more great books to read, not to mention the Holy Scripture itself.

But it was his own countryman, the Irishman Brendan whom Aedan kept returning to again and again. *He* was a priest, thought Aedan, and yet an adventurer, too! Seaman and scholar: it was proof to Aedan that both worlds could be compatible. A man could be pious and loyal to his church, but also adventurous and curious about the temporal world. He wanted to be a Brendan as well, an intrepid sailor traveling to the farthest reaches of the vast watery round sphere that was earth, encountering whatever strange peoples inhabited those outer corners.

And why not? He was, after all, the true, biological son of the great Spanish seaman and wine merchant Jacobo de Adamo, though within St. Alban's walls, he was simply Aedan, a boy without a family name, a foundling and official ward of the priests. Lord Fulke was, in essence, his true father, the man who had raised him and educated him with a cool, muted affection. Aedan had only learned in recent years of his real father, who did not reside in Ireland and had never married his mother, who'd died shortly after Aedan's birth. But as Aedan grew into manhood, he was becoming convinced that his natural father's love of the sea and passion for exploration ran in his own blood as well.

Fulke and his priests had not expected much from this boy who had been dropped on their stone steps as an infant, shrieking and crying in a rough fisherman's basket. Through some inquiry and gossip, they learned the boy was the child of a poor Inis Ghall lass, a clam-gatherer's daughter who died in childbed—though some islanders said she'd died from pure shame, when the dashing Spanish nobleman she'd had fallen in love with in Galway would not take her as his wife. The identity of the father did not emerge until de Adamo himself came looking for the boy, some ten years later. It was not known who dropped the baby off or why they chose Galway's tiniest church. St. Alban's had been founded by an English-Norman sect called the Albanites, a group who valued books and education but had little wealth or influence. The little church, housed in what had been a former Norse fortress and compound near the western gate of the city, lay practically in the shadows of Galway's mighty cathedral, Saint Nicholas of Myra.

Aedan had spent his entire life within St. Alban's gray limestone walls, newly rebuilt after the disastrous Galway fire of 1475. He was not forbidden to leave or wander the city streets, but he saw little reason to do so. He rarely left the abbey, except when his natural father came into port.

Somehow Jacobo de Adamo had learned of his son's existence: Galway was a small city, a haven for gossip. He made inquiries and tracked Aedan down at St. Alban's. Aedan, then a boy of ten, had been frightened of the burly Spaniard at first, with his thick black beard, piercing eyes and direct manner. But de Adamo told Aedan that he had indeed loved his mother, but that he was already married. And that wealthy, bejeweled Portuguese wife in Madeira was barren, unable to bear him an heir, so Aedan was his only child. Aedan did not dare ask why his father would seek out another woman in Ireland, when he already had a wife. But there was no doubt in his mind that de Adamo was indeed his father. Aedan saw it in the man's face, in the narrow jawline and long aquiline nose they both shared, even though Aedan's coloring came from his mother, hair streaked gold and amber, eyes the blue-green color of a sunny Mediterranean bay, though overscored with a darkish, Iberian brow.

Aedan had grown fond of de Adamo and looked forward to his visits from Madeira. The Normans of Galway were quite fond of this sweet wine from the distant Portuguese isle, so Jacobo traveled frequently to the Irish port with a plentiful supply from his own fields and grapes to sell. Jacobo was intelligent, engaging, a bit of a dandy in his velvet and silk doublets and hose, but a man's man, impressive in stature, with a deep hearty laugh that seemed to bubble constantly into his conversations. Everything seemed to amuse him—the world in general, the provinciality and backwardness of Galway folk, the snobbishness of the English priests. Though Aedan's life at St. Alban's was not unhappy, Jacobo's visits were something to look forward to, bursts of color, sunny chaos and laughter amid the grayness of Galway's frequently foggy days.

Aedan was thinking of him now, even as he studied his Brendan-map and manuscripts, for alongside the books was one of his father's portulan maps, a simple line drawing done in Jacobo's hand, showing the various ports he had called at. The line stretched from Morroque in northern Africa to Lisbon and Biscay and then to Bristol in England and Galway, then slightly beyond, north to the Faeroes and Shetlands. A small line strayed to Iceland then went no further.

The last time Jacobo came to visit, he discussed his home and fields in Madeira, an island in the Western Sea close to Africa. It had only been discovered decades before, but was already filling up with settlers, sugar-cane and wine-grape farmers from Portugal and Spain. Jacobo had acquired a fine estate there and was building a great manse; his wife was already living there. The climate, he said, was heavenly: Always summer, balmy breezes and blue skies.

What other marvelous isles lay in the west sea that had not yet been discovered? Aedan wondered, as he rolled up his scrolls and put aside the map-books. He longed to know, and visit them.

And then, in one of those strange events that occur sometimes in ordinary life, just as he was thinking about his father, old Brother Paulus stomped in to announce Jacobo's arrival in the visitors' hall.

"It's the wayward Spaniard again, here to make trouble for ye," he muttered. If Lord Fulke served as Aedan's genteel father, then Paulus was his lovable and cantankerous older uncle. A native of Connemarra's wild country, he had taught Aedan a number of Irish songs and stories as well as the *Gaeilge* tongue itself, which was forbidden not only within St. Alban's but in all of Galway city, where the Norman conquerers' English was decreed by law.

"I'd send him on his way, with a kick in the arse. If it t'were up to me..."

Aedan grinned. "I always value your advice, Brother Paulus." He hurried out into the corridor toward the visitors' room.

In the hallway, Lord Fulke reached out and plucked at his sleeve. Fulke was a tall man, reaching nearly six feet, though his student Aedan was now within an inch of him. He was reedy, balding, with fog-gray eyes that gave him a distant look.

"Remember, son: Your father is a man of the world, a sinful world. You are meant for something better. " He paused, pursing his lips. "Do not let him take you down into the city this time."

But within moments, Aedan and his father Jacobo were cheerfully strolling past the gates of the abbey, into the hilly rabbit-warren of alleys that was Galway. A walled city, it continued to grow and prosper almost claustrophobically within the limestone rock that encircled it, despite invasions, constant clashes between English lords and native Irish, and the occasional plague or fire.

Aedan was always amazed at how well his father, a foreigner, knew the city. Jacobo always knew where the best inns were, the best taverns and how to avoid the crooks and highwaymen who lingered by the port and the gates of the city. Today he escorted Aedan to a quieter, less raucous sort of inn, taking a table in a darkish corner, indicating that he had something serious to discuss.

"You're looking well, boy. A bit thin." Jacobo now spoke in a mixture of Basque and Spanish: he had been born in the Navarre region of Spain, and his father had been of Castillian, and noble, blood. But his mother was Basque and fiercely proud of her heritage. She taught Jacobo her *Euskera* language before teaching him proper Spanish, and Jacobo had shared this unusual tongue with Aedan as well. It was the language of fishermen and seafarers, Jacobo told him, and could be useful to him one day. So now Aedan—who fortunately was adept at language—spoke two secret tongues, *Gaeilge* and *Euskera*. The Basque was a language the priests and other Irishmen could not understand, and it added a layer of intimacy to his relationship with Jacobo.

"What do those damned priests *feed* you? You need meat, good meat, and plenty of bread. You're a handsome lad, you know, with my features and your mother's coloring. I could see the lasses taking a hard look at you as we were walking down here."

Aedan turned crimson, but grinned. He'd seen the girls, too, but did not know what to make of them. He felt himself drawn to them, curious, wanting to talk to them, but a little terrified as well.

The entire female sex seemed a foreign race to him, a great tantalizing mystery, for he had known neither mother nor sisters. The priests did not talk of them; in fact, they acted as if the world was filled only with men. Aedan did not even dare to ask Lord Fulke how *not* to be so curious and intrigued about them; or how to keep those images of pretty maidens from poking into serious prayers and Scripture study.

"You think you can live without girls?" Jacobo asked, with a wink, as if guessing Aedan's thoughts. Once again Aedan found himself burning with embarrassment, but did not reply.

"I shouldn't question the Lord Fulke's plans for you," said Jacobo in a contrite way. "He is raising you to manhood, not I. And the priesthood is a fine enough profession, plenty of wealth and power if you manage to rise to bishop, or cardinal. You *could* have a good life here. But rather dull, I think, chained to one church, one place. Do you ever think," he began in a casual way, "about seeing the rest of the world? Becoming a man of the sea, like myself?"

At this Aedan's heart began to pound. "I do think of it, Father. Sometimes. As you know I have a great interest in the world and in sailing. But I have never even been on board a ship! I'm not sure I would be suited for it."

"Some men aren't. You need a strong constitution for the sea. A strong stomach, for the food is bad, and the waves themselves will sicken you at times. Then there is the peril of boredom, of being becalmed, long days waiting for wind or current…Ah, I have something for you, a little gift." He handed Aedan a small flat object wrapped in gossamer linen. Aedan eagerly unwrapped it, then held the odd object to the light.

It was some sort of clam or mussel shell: A strange shape, like the wing of a falcon, and rough grayish-black on one side. But inside, a true rainbow of colors glistened, even in the dim candle-lit interior of the inn.

"It's beautiful," he whispered. "Is it the fabled pearl-oyster?"

"It is indeed."

"It's not from European waters, is it?"

"Europe has its pearls, but nothing like this. The gems that royal lords and ladies wear come mainly from the Orient, the Indies to the far east."

"Is that where this shell comes from? Where did you get it?"

"From this crazy Basque guy, a whaler I met at the port. He sold me no pearls, but several sacks of these shells. They're almost as valuable. See, they can be made into buttons, or other ornaments."

"That Basque…reached the Orient?"

Jacobo laughed. "I doubt it, although he'd probably claim he had. Urraco Vizkiero, that's his name—half whaler, half pirate. The Basques are an honest race, but he gives them a bad name. Old Urraco led me to believe he'd collected these himself, but I know better. Likely he and his gang waylaid a ship coming round off the Horn of Africa, and took their goods. I shouldn't have bought them, but…" He sighed. "It doesn't hurt to try and make a little extra money. For my old age."

Aedan was alarmed by those words: Old age. Was Jacobo planning to give up his life at sea? And so, his frequent visits to Galway? He studied his father gravely: Jacobo *was* getting old, lots of gray strands now in his dark beard and hair.

"So tell me," Jacobo continued, on a more jovial note, "Do you know anything about this so-called *mermaid* who supposedly washed ashore on your native island?"

"A mermaid? On Inis Ghall?" Aedan was startled. He was rational enough to know such creatures were pure myth and did not truly exist, even if they were occasionally depicted on maps. And the very thought of one, a woman whose nether regions descended into a shimmering net of fish scales, suddenly delighted and tormented him.

"Indeed!" Jacobo broke into a lusty laugh, seeing his son so flustered. "You Irish are hilarious! Seeing little spirits in the woods and grasses. Imagining fair maidens who turn themselves into birds, fish, other creatures—"

"Seals. Those would be selkies. The mermaids, they call *maruch mhara*." Aedan recalled some of Brother Paulus' stories, about these unusual females. He suspected Paulus actually believed in such things.

"Selkie, siren, mermaid...It was a probably just a girl, a human girl. But dark as a chestnut, they say, with raven-black hair. Washed up with the tides, dead or alive, I have no idea. They say she appears, and disappears. That's all I know of the story, and the man who told me was a drunken fisherman, by the port."

"Drunk, eh? That explains it."

"But there's a grain of truth in it, I'm thinking." Jacobo's eyes were merry and challenging.

"There are no mermaids, Father. Or have you seen some, on your travels?" Aedan teased him back.

Jacobo roared with laughter. "Alas, no sirens or mermaids. But I've seen many women. Many *strange* women, and some quite bewitching, I tell you!"

Aedan leaned back, wanting desperately to turn the conversation away from the troublesome subject of girls and women. He caressed the glistening silver-touched shell in his hand. Pearls, the Basque, a strange dark woman washing ashore in Inis Ghall...

"Father, have you ever sailed west of here? Far west?"

"To Madeira, of course. And once, and only once, to godforsaken Iceland, north and west. "

"Beyond that."

Jacobo chortled. "There's nothing out there, son!"

"Are you sure of that?"

"Don't tell me you've been dreaming over your maps again! Reading that crazy Brendan! Don't you have anything better to do? Listen, this is what lies west—" He counted off the lands on his thick fingers. "The Azores and the Dog Islands—the Canaries. To the north, Iceland, where you go to trade for cod and furs and such. Northern ivory. Then there is a big Norse island just beyond that. The idiots call it 'Greenland' but it is nothing but frozen waste. So I am told. And some Basques say a land lies beyond that, they call it Codland. But you can't really believe a thing those damned whalers tell you."

"What about Hy-Brasil?" Aedan asked. "The Isle of the Blessed, said to lie far out in the Western Sea?"

"No such place."

"It's on all the maps."

"Your maps lie."

"They don't!" Aedan retorted, alarmed at his father's irreverence. "Why would a respectable mapmaker set down an imaginary island?"

"To sell their maps. They all copy from one another, you know."

"I think there is something more out there, undiscovered land to the west of here."

"There are islands," said Jacobo with a shrug, "So small and flat that they only appear when the tide favors them. That's your Hy-Brasil."

"If you sailed west far enough, wouldn't you reach the Orient? The islands of Cipangu and Cathay?"

"Cathay!" Jacobo roared. "That's nonsense!"

"Is it? Why? If the world is indeed a sphere — as some men suggest — and if you sailed long enough, wouldn't you eventually reach the Far East?"

"And if you continued to keep sailing west, you'd end up back in Ireland. Of course it's *possible*, if you had the best ships and all the time in the world. But you would run out of food and fresh water before you got there. You would reach Cathay, but you would be dead."

21

"It's the distance, then. A problem of time." Aedan wondered over this. How long would it take to cross the western ocean? Months? Years? His father was telling him he might as well try to fly and reach the moon.

"But Saint Brendan did it," he said, softly, obstinate. "He wrote of it –"

"Brendan!" His father's tone turned contemptuous. "You and your fairy tale books! I tell you as a seaman, there's not a word of truth to that old fable!"

"It's the work of a *saint!* He would not *lie!*"

"In all my years of sailing, I have never even seen one of the so-called wonders he describes in those stories of his! Monsters forging steel, and crystal-diamond columns rising out of the sea…Hah! I think that tale is the invention of a bored monk!"

"I cannot believe," said Aedan, in a smoldering tone, "That my brilliant teachers would allow us to read a text that was untrue, full of lies---"

"Then come with me!" Jacobo exploded. "Come with me, son, and see for yourself! Let me teach you what I know. Abandon your womanish life behind the walls of St. Alban's and see the world as it really is, not portrayed – falsely – in books and manuscripts."

"Come…come with you?" Aedan whispered. It was as if Jacobo had asked him to enter the Gates of Hell. Impossible, outrageous…and perversely, so tempting.

"This is my last voyage north," Jacobo said, gravely. "I am getting old now and stiff in my joints. I can't sail much more. But if you come with me now, I can teach you, tell you what I know. You are my blood, my heir. You could take over my property and business when I die, and sail the world yourself. Visit the great ports, the Mediterranean...think of the exotic, beautiful girls you could meet!"

Aedan gaped at him. "Leave? Leave St. Alban's? I cannot!"

"Madeira!" Jacobo crowed. "It is the isle of the future! That is your paradise, your Hy-Brasil! It's warm, heavenly all year round, no snow or ice. A great rich fertile mountain of island, teased by tropical breezes. There are plenty of families there now, beautiful girls from Portugal and Spain! It's a good place for a young man."

"I am committed to the priesthood, Lord Fulke says I am, he says it is the only hope for my salvation, a poor foundling, born into sin—"

"You are my son," said Jacobo, firmly and gently. "I was wrong not to take you away with me years ago, when I first discovered you. I should have brought you to Madeira then but I was afraid of offending my wife, I did not know how to explain you to her...I was weak, and I curse myself for that now. But it is not too late...You can come with me now."

"When do you leave?" Aedan actually felt weak at the knees, at the thought of such a daring move. To throw away everything he had studied and worked for—and perhaps his immortal soul as well! But what a reward, what an adventure it would be!

23

"Tomorrow! At dawn."

Aedan swallowed. How could he possibly explain to Lord Fulke that he was abandoning him and the Church, leaving for what was likely to be a worldly, Satanish sort of life, after so many years of study and prayer?

"In truth, Father, I am torn. I would like to go with you, I've come to love you as my true father, and I want to take my place with you. I'm curious to see the world beyond Eire, that's true. But on the other hand, St. Alban's is the only home I've ever known. I feel I owe Lord Fulke an enormous debt for taking me in and not allowing me to die, and for guiding and teaching me all these years. It will be a tremendous blow to him and the others should I leave."

"You have a night to sleep on it. Gather your things, and meet me at my ship at dawn. If you are not there, then I will sail nevertheless." He sighed deeply. "I can't force you against your will. But as a father who has only one son in the world, no other progeny to share in my life and my wealth, I beg you to come. I will give you my name, and my undying fatherly love."

Aedan de Adamo. A true name, and a noble one! It was something to consider.

Aedan trudged alone back up to St. Alban's with enormous sadness. Whatever decision he made would make someone he cared about very unhappy. And he wasn't sure which decision would make himself happy.

He knelt at prayer with the priests in the hours before dawn, trying to immerse himself in the holy chant. But he could only think about his father and what he was offering him. The lures of the outside world, Lord Fulke warned him time and again, were false, fleeting. Better, he said, to invest one's time and energy in preparing for the world to come then to exhaust oneself in the current one.

But he *wanted* to go! He *so* wanted to go! Could the Almighty really be so very angry at him if he just spent a few years with his father, tasting what the world had to offer? And then he could come back to his holy life, and spend the rest of his days atoning for whatever pleasures he'd had outside the church's walls. How could he truly know what sin was, if he never had the chance to commit one?

As the sky began to lighten, his thoughts turned desperate. He had to leave, he had to leave *now*. *Go now!* He commanded himself, and yet his legs would not rise, his feet would not carry him out of the chapel. Around him the drone of men's voices in serious prayer continued, and the colored glazed windows of the church glowed with the coming day.

He remained on his knees well through dawn, and sat down to his repast of dark dry bread and weakened wine, feeling enormous regret and sadness, knowing the time for his escape had passed. He felt neither relieved nor proud of his decision. He felt, unmistakably, like a weakling, a coward...a bad son.

3.

She awoke to darkness, and the shrill sound of screaming. But not the screams of men: Birds, sea birds, thousands of them massed just outside the cave where she lay recovering from the fever she'd caught from her captors. It was a frightful thing, that illness, like nothing she had ever experienced before, a burning within her, and a constricting sense in her lungs, a feeling she could not draw breath.

It had killed some of those men, those sailors who had stolen her from her home. But others had survived. And she knew it would not kill her: She was stronger in body than they were.

She blinked in the darkness of the cave, not really sure if she were still asleep, dreaming, or awake. Had she passed into the netherworld beyond death? She knew only that she was indeed in some new kind of world, a different place than the one she had been born into and raised. And in this new world, it was *cold*.

She had no idea how she had come to be in this cave, but she was grateful for the shelter of it, and also for the flame-haired boy, the child who brought her food and fibers to keep her warm. He came for several days in a row, but had not come back since the sun had set the night before.

He called her *Marra*. It was not her true name, the name her mother and father had given her. But that girl no longer existed. She was a new person in this new land; she accepted this name she had been given, though it made no sense to her. In her captors' language, *Marra* meant pole or line, something straight and rigid. It was also the sound a cat made, a small creature she had never seen until she was taken aboard her captors' ship. It hunted the mice and rats that had plagued the vessel, then came up to the deck to cry and purr in satisfaction.

She lay on a bed of long, stiff grasses, covered by a foul-smelling woven cloth. She surmised she was in some kind of cave by the sea, owing to the overwhelming sea smell of salt and fish. Her curiosity about her new surrounding was dulled by the wracking pain in her limbs, and the laborious process of trying to breath. But she would live.

In her endless tossing and turning, she saw her father's face, his kind eyes and weathered skin. It wavered before her as if had all those times when she would be swimming up from the ocean depths, and he above her, looking down from his canoe. His arms reaching out for her...

Instinctively she reached for the pearl, the perfect pearl, about her neck. It was still there and she felt a tiny comfort in its cool smoothness. She tried again, to summon her father's face.

But this time, she saw, quick as a flash, her captors tossing her father's body overboard, letting him sink into the cold, dark sea.

Father, she whispered now, using her captors' word: *Aita.*

She'd had many months to learn their tongue and she had worked at it that entire horrible winter on that creaking, ceaselessly rocking ship. It had occupied her mind, keeping her terror at bay. She learned their language, so she could outwit them, and escape.

And she had. Only to end up in this state, this cave, more dead than alive. From time to time the boy had forced brackish water down her throat, and vile food into her mouth: Rancid meat she could not identify and some strange paste, similar to the cassava-cake the women of her island made, but with a lumpier texture and no flavor whatsoever. She would creak her eyes open slightly, to see a pale freckled face, blue eyes and hair the color of fire. *Koe-lum*, the boy called himself.

He was one of the pale ones, her captors' race. People of a cold land, in reeking soiled garments filled with lice. Barely civilized, she'd thought.

"Ur—" she had croaked to the boy once, her throat as parched as beach sand. "*Urgeza*," she tried to tell him, clutching her throat for emphasis. *Water.* The boy had not understood. Perhaps he was feeble-minded.

Another time she imagined someone else hovering over her, a crone with rheumy eyes and a pinched mouth. A bony finger descended, to touch the pearl at her neck. The death goddess, perhaps, and Marra feared her return.

The fever flared up again and again, searing her skin from inside, closing her throat. She shut her eyes and the sun of her native island was hot upon skin once again, mid-summer sun in a cloudless sky. The white sand beneath her feet burned with it, as she walked down to the turquoise lagoon where her father sat in his canoe.

Come, daughter, it's a good day for finding pearls.

She hadn't wanted to go, still tired from the day before. They had been fishing out beyond the reef and a summer storm had come in. It took enormous effort to return the little dugout to their lagoon. They had brought back few clams, and none had contained pearls.

We will find some today, said her father. Many fat clams, many pearls.

She could not refuse her father. He was all she had, no other family. Years before, wild tribes from the south, the *Caribe*, had attacked their island, killing her mother and brothers and many others as well. She had been just a small girl then, already learning to dive for pearl-clams with her father. They had been out in the ocean when it happened and returned to find the dead littering the beach. Each time they returned from pearl-fishing, she half-expected to come home to some similar shock or horror, although the tribes from the south had never returned. Out in the ocean, she would scan the waves, looking for their canoes and painted scarified faces, terrified they would come back for her and her father after all these years.

She waded out into the warm waters of the lagoon, brilliant green against the backdrop of white-sand beach and deep blue ocean. Swarms of little fish and fronds of seagrass circled her legs as she waded out to her father's canoe. They paddled though the little break in the reef they knew so well, and out into the great plain of darker water that was the open ocean.

Urgeza, she whispered again: Not a plea for drinking water, but a soft lament, longing for the sea, her sea. Then she remembered: *Urgeza* meant fresh water. *Urgazi* was water from the sea. *Itsaso* meant the sea itself...

Koe-lum had seemed puzzled by her words. She recalled now that he seemed to speak a strange, garbled language of his own. She had been unable to pick out a single recognizable word. She realized now that he spoke a different language than that spoken by her captors.

So, she was not in the land of her captors. But where could she be?

A shadow darkened the opening of the cave. Marra turned her eyes, hoping to see the brilliant fire-hair of the boy Koe-lum. But she saw a more frightening vision, the old death-crone now stalking her, coming for her. Her bony hands went to Marra's neck, and Marra screamed into the darkness, unwilling to be snatched from earth so soon...

4.

Only days after discovering the raven-dark maiden on the sandy beach near the pagans' caves, Colm began to cough. He felt a dry soreness in his throat and a buzzing warmness in his head. He felt so dizzy, he could not leave the sleeping pallet of hay and straw he shared with his little sister, Itta, and his mother tended to him with mutton broth and herbs, her face creased with worry. Itta, too, became mysteriously feverish, lapsing into long periods of stuporous sleep.

When both children rose, their fever broken, it was to find their father, Inis Ghall's priest, deathly ill himself, hot with fever. Their mother was missing.

Father Comgall, the pastor of Inis Ghall's tumbledown stone church, now lay helpless in his corner of hay, his face bright red and ablaze with fever. Colm, still woozy with the illness, inched toward him.

"Where is Mam?" he asked, in a fearful voice, and his father could only summon enough strength to point to the door. The little family lived in a small room behind the sanctuary of the church itself. Colm creaked open the batten door and

31

there, just outside, was a rough wooden coffin, a body bound in strips of linen. He saw a wisp of his mother's blonde hair escaping from the shroud. Numbed, in shock, Colm touched the hair; the body beneath felt cold to his touch.

"Oh, Mam..." he whispered.

How could she be dead, his beautiful young story-telling mother? How could she have died so quickly? He felt he would die, too, of sheer grief. Would the evil fever now take his father as well?

It is my fault, he thought in horror: For saving the dark girl he'd called *mhara* — of the sea. She had been ill, he thought, and now she had infected them all with her illness.

Since the priest could not rise from his sickbed, neighbors came to take his mother's body. She had to be buried quickly, without a Mass or prayers. Colm went with the neighbor and helped dig the grave, but looked away when she was lowered in, reciting the prayers for the dead in his head.

The neighbor told Colm that several other islanders had come down with a similar fever, and that Donnacha, the eel-fisher married to the beachcomber Anhin, was staggering about, raving about a 'black witch' who had cursed the island. He was thought to be senile, but the outbreak of serious illness had everyone worried.

"Could be plague," the neighbor mused. "Coming in from Galway, maybe on a cloud or wind. All those foreigners coming and going...who knows?"

It was not clear if Father Comgall would survive his ordeal. Though most of his flock were simple, uneducated farmers and fishermen, they also knew the pope in Rome had forbidden his priests to marry and have families. Though they were sympathetic to their priest, unable to understand distant Rome's harsh pronouncement against the natural course of love, they predicted the defiant Comgall would die, quickly and painfully, as punishment for breaking his vows.

It fell to Colm to do the chores his mother had done, to keep his father and sister alive. Most importantly, he had to forage for food. This was a difficult task in early spring, when nothing yet sprouted from the earth, and root-cellars were empty.

He wandered down to the western shore, casting only a cursory glance in the direction of the raven-girl's cave. Bitterly, he hoped she had died there, for all the misery she had caused him. He continued on, remembering that his mother sometimes boiled snails with seaweeds, when nothing else was available. He could also search the cave cliff for puffin eggs, which were tasty when roasted on the coals.

He paused by the seaside stone hut that belonged to Anhin and Donnacha. No smoke poured from their chimney and there was no noise from within.

"Anhin! Old woman, come out!" he shouted. But there was no answer.

He creaked open the door, only to see a sorry sight: Anhin and Donnacha lay side by side on their pallet of straw, still as cut tree logs. Covering his mouth, Colm inched into the hut.

Apparently the deadly fever came on quickly. Donnacha's freshly caught eels still wriggled vigorously in a pail of water by the door. Colm roughly pulled down the neckline of Anhin's shift, and as he suspected, saw the raven-girl's pearl hidden there in the wrinkles of her neck. He carefully undid the knot in the string of strange fiber—neither linen nor wool—and took the pearl from her. She had no need for it now.

He then took her cloak, from a peg on the wall. It was perhaps the only decent thing she owned, for all her decades of beachcombing, a dun-brown swath of wool from the island's sheep, woven on the mainland. He glanced at the wriggling eels— he would come back for those later. But right now, he had another task.

He had to go and appease the raven girl. He knew that she must have been angered by the theft of her precious pearl; that was why she continued to send her illness to all the people who lived in Inis Ghall.

He made his way toward the cliff caves, shivering inwardly. He would give her the pearl back, and the warm cloak as well. Perhaps then she would spare his father and the other islanders.

High tide roared against the boulders at the western point; the sea birds screamed and cawed above. He climbed up and peered into the cave, but to his surprise, did not see her. Had she escaped, so soon? But then he heard a cooing from above—

"Kooooo-lum! Koe-lum!"

She sat perched on the ledge just above him, seeming neither displeased nor threatening, just a young dark-skinned lass in a dirty cream-linen shift, her long bare legs dangling, her black hair blowing in the wind. She held out her hand to him, but he took a step backwards. She laughed, as if nervous, confused.

"Koe-lum?"

Keeping a good few feet between them, he handed up to her Anhin's cloak. With pantomiming gestures, he showed her how to wrap it around herself, drawing it tight around the neck, and she nodded, grateful, immediately donning it.

Then he dangled the pearl to her. At this her face lit up with pure joy and she uttered a small cry as she reached for and took it.

He darted away now, without a glance back. He had done his job, he had made the dark maiden happy. Perhaps now she would swim off and leave the island alone.

Perhaps now his father would live.

He brought home the eels and cooked them as best he could, boiling them in the one big kettle his mother kept on the hearth. He cut the eel meat into smooth circles, but could not get his father to eat, only drink the salty cooking broth from the kettle. But little Itta, just three years old, eagerly consumed the eel circles as if she had never been sick at all.

Later that night, by the fireside, unable to sleep, Colm lit the grease-lamp and took out one of his boards. Colm liked to draw and sketch, though he had no parchment nor quill. It was a frivolous talent that his father, seemed to encourage. He called it "art" and said men on the continent of Europe became famous for it, and perhaps Colm would too one day. Colm liked to draw imaginary battle scenes and hounds and horses, but now he began a sketch of a woman: His mother, Orlaith. He wanted to remember, when he was old, what she looked like. He never wanted to forget her face.

But as he drew, with a piece of charred wood, another face emerged as if his hand were being guided by some other force. He found himself drawing the raven girl with her black, black hair and coal-dark eyes.

"No!" he cried aloud. Disconsolate, he tossed the board aside.

From outside the church building, he though he heard a noise, a rustling in the currant-bushes that ringed the church. He blew out the grease-lamp and peered out the doorway. From the tiny settlement or *clachan* surrounding the church, from one of the wattled huts came a wail and a scream. The fever had claimed yet another victim.

5.

She was asleep now, deep into the night. Inside her cave, she felt snug in the wool cape the boy had brought her, the pearl safely back on her neck. She was dreaming, back on her native island.

Her father was speaking to her, about marrying:

You are old enough now. More than old enough, seventeen summers, and you should have a husband by now, children of your own. I am an old man. We can't do this pearl-fishing much longer, you and I.

I don't want a man or babies now! I won't give up pearl-fishing, I'm good at it! I want to stay with you as long as I can and fish with you.

It's not normal for a grown-up girl to stay with her father. And I won't always be here. It would make me feel better, if you found a mate. I will choose one for you.

There aren't any boys on the island that I like well enough.

Then we will find another island.

They were in the canoe, just sitting there, the waves and wind calm. Her father often chose such times to discuss important matters with her. But the conversation ended when he tied the twined palm-rope around her waist, and she picked up the clam-basket, diving into the cool, deep-blue waters. She kicked her feet and dove deeper into the ocean depths, carefully holding her breath as her father had taught her. Slowly, slowly, not too quickly, she let herself sink to the bottom of the sea. She felt no fear, but rather a giddy sort of euphoria, a sense that she had become part fish, a creature of the sea: A dangerous sensation because she almost believed she could inhale the sea as if it were air.

The sea bottom was thick that day with black pearl clams. They liked barren areas of the sea bed without coral or plants, and they tethered themselves to the muddy bottom with their magical thin threads, like plants setting out roots. She pulled at them, tugging them from their moorings, filling her basket until the warning tug from her father came. Then she rose to the surface with her bounty.

He had laughed aloud when he saw the clams she picked: They were huge, glistening, beautiful oysters, promising all sorts of riches. Later they would crack open the clams and roast their tender delicious flesh on the coals of the fire. Some would contain precious pearls for trading. And perhaps there might be one spectacular pearl, like the one she had found earlier in the year: Not white or gray like the others, but a pale gold bordering on pink, like the last rays of sun before night. She had been so taken with it, she begged her father not to trade it away but to let her wear it on a string of twisted cotton. He had patiently drilled a hole through its core with a sliver of flint and she wore it proudly, a sign of her special status as the daughter of the pearl-fisher.

She dove back into the sea that day for more. They had been too greedy, she would reflect later, she and her father. The sea gods had been displeased. She had taken too many of the pearl-clams. That was the only reason she could come up with for what happened next, just after she collected what would be the last full basket of clams.

If only she had known! She would have stayed under the waters and breathed in the cool sea water like air, never to rise again.

She felt the warning tug of rope at her waist and she began to rise, with some impatience. Her father continued to tug in a relentless way. She didn't understand why, and reacted with annoyance, when she surfaced.

What is it? she'd snapped, rubbing at the newly raw spot on her waist where the twine had burned. Her father's back was to her, he did not speak. She dumped her clams into the canoe, then looked at him again. Something in the way he sat there, rigid, frozen, instantly terrified her.

Father? What is it? What are you looking at?

He was staring at the horizon, to the east.

Was it a swarm of sharks? She hoped it was that, and only that. You could swim away, outwit a shark. But men in canoes and boats, that was a different matter. She pulled herself into the canoe and followed her father's stare.

There, atop the waves in the distance, was what she thought was a giant bird or cormorant: Great pale flapping wings, not soaring above but gliding on the surface of the sea. Coming toward them, swiftly. Her father began to paddle the canoe to shore, his movements stiff with shock and fright. The little dugout was low in the water, unwieldy with its load of pearl-clams. Frantically, she began to throw handfuls of the clams overboard to lighten the load, but it wasn't enough. The strange bird or creature was overshadowing them now. There was no escape.

What is it? She whispered to her father. He kept his face averted from hers.

It's a vessel, a boat, he had murmured. *A large boat, filled with pale men.*

She awoke in a sweat-soaked terror, screaming. When she stopped, she still heard the screams echoing in her ears, but then remembered the flocks of sea birds, outside the cave.

She needed to escape: She was beginning to hate this lonely cave and the constant darkness; she needed to walk, to run, to feel the wind in her hair. She emerged into the twilight, the rising golden moon looking unfamiliar and alien to her, even if it were the same moon that shined down on her at home. She now fully realized she had not passed into the death-world, but was still alive, under the same moon and stars and sun, but in a different, distant, part of world.

And what a strange world it was! It could indeed be the world of the dead, so bleak and colorless compared to her native isle. There were no jungles, no trees, no colorful parrots or flowers or fruits, nor iguanas, scorpions nor many insects at all. Even the sea itself was a dead gray-greenish color, so cold it numbed her feet after only a few moments contact. There were no coral reefs, no yellow and blue fish, and the shells this sea spit forth were chalky and gray. The pearl clams, she thought, would not live here.

Gingerly, she climbed down the cliff-side to the shore, the sand wet and cold beneath her feet. Stripping the flat limpets off the rocks with a quick flick of her fingernail, she devoured the raw, salty morsels. She cracked open several sea urchins, scooping out the ochre substance inside. She was still alive, she needed to eat. Huddled in her brown cape, she then began to venture up shore, feeling cloaked as well by the coming night. She wanted to explore this odd place without attracting the attention of its inhabitants. She trusted only the red-haired boy, but he had not come back now in several days, not since returning her pearl.

She trudged up to the dunes and swathes of sea grass, gazing out into the night landscape. She thought she saw, in the distance, the light of fires, outlines of roofs and huts, perhaps a small settlement of people. This was perhaps where Koelum lived, and she felt a spark of curiosity.

She would go and investigate, carefully, secretly. They must not see her; she could not let herself be captured again. But she needed to know what sort of people she had been set down amongst. She needed to learn about them, as she had learned about her captors. Only then could she stay ahead of them, and outwit them if she needed to.

A hard truth had come to her: She could not go *home*. She would never be returning home. She did not even know where home was anymore, only that it lay to the west and south somewhere, the place where the sun sank at night. But she could never return there: The sea was too vast, too big. And she could not remember the way back.

She had to learn how to live here, how to survive in this cold, odd land. And so she began to make her way across the flat meadows, alert but furtive, crouched down and ready to flee, at any moment, into bushes or shadows. She would not be caught again.

6.

Galway was small city, and it didn't take long for word of the Inis Ghall creature to reach the walls of St. Alban's. The priests and brothers heard that residents of the hapless isle seemed to be dying of a fever-plague, ever since a strange dark-haired girl had been found in the surf there. She was said to be a creature of the sea, a *murúch* or mermaid.

The story set off a fierce debate among the scholars. The more educated men, including Lord Fulke, did not believe a word of it, dismissing the girl as an unfortunate African or Asian slave who had fallen off a passing ship. Certainly a female of dubious morals, they sniffed, not worthy of any kind of serious consideration.

But old Brother Paulus swore the story must be true, asserting that the fishermen of Inis Ghall were an honest lot, not known for creating fanciful tales. And the ancient writers had mentioned such creatures, hadn't they? He had no doubt about what sort of being had infiltrated the Foreigner's Isle: An actual fish-tailed, fish-scaled mermaid!

This in turn set off a completely new debate among the priests and their guests, young and old, educated and simple, at a mealtime when they were free to converse. If such a creature did exist, half woman, half fish, was she a human being?

someone asked. Did she have an immortal soul, a chance at redemption and eternal life?

"Never mind that it's part fish!" snarled one grizzled friar, visiting from across town. "It's a *female*, and none of those creatures have any soul!"

Fulke frowned at him. "You are insulting Our Lady and all the great female saints, brother Tadgh. You know perfectly well women are capable of great intelligence and piety. And they have souls as do men." In contrast to many of his fellow priests, Fulke was a nobleman, born into wealth, polite but intimidating. His speech and his bearing betrayed his aristocratic, Norman ancestry and he spoke only Latin or English, never the local Galway dialect of Irish, which he professed not to understand.

"If she is more than fifty-one percent human," one of the scholars intoned. "That is, if only a small part of her body is…human, as if were, then she is capable of possessing a soul. But if she be more animal than human—"

"Don't be ridiculous!" another shouted. "We're arguing about something that doesn't exist, except in the mind of some demented fisherman!"

Aedan followed the conversation eagerly, immensely curious about the girl who had washed ashore on his native island.

"Raven-black her hair is, and skin the color of roasted hazelnuts in autumn," Paulus had told him. "Or so I've heard. They say at night she runs about like any lass with two legs, but during the day takes her fish form. "

Aedan was still grieving his decision not to sail with his father Jacobo, but several weeks had passed, and the pain and regret were fading. He distracted himself with his studies and his maps. Now, this new and intriguing news from Inis Ghall gave him much to ponder.

The idea of a *murúch* seemed fantastic, unbelievable, but he had read of strange races of humans who lived to the east and the south. There were woodcuts of these creatures on the margins of the maps he studied, deformed men with the manes of lions or a single eye positioned in the center of their foreheads. There were men who ate other men! Why would scholars write about such things, if there were not some kind of truth attached to it? And for what purpose would the Lord create such people, and didn't he love and care for them as well as his 'normal' men of Europe and Asia?

"Perhaps," he ventured, shyly, the student from the low end of the table, "this creature, whatever she is, needs to be converted to our faith. Baptized."

The others turned to him. Aedan was a quiet boy, not known for spouting off or making outlandish statements, highly regarded for his intense scholarship and respectful loyalty to Lord Fulke.

"It is not an insensible idea," Fulke drawled, pleased with his ward's observation. "I imagine the local prelate was too dim to think of it. Who is the pastor there?"

"It's this clown, Comgall, I knew him at seminary," another of the priests spoke up. "He is said to be something of an apostate, and allegedly has a woman living in his quarters."

Fulke tsk-tsked.

"Many of them out in Connemarra still follow the ways of the old church," Brother Paulus remarked. "Marrying and having families of their own. It seems natural to them."

"But it is against the rules of our modern Church," said Fulke sternly. "If nothing else, someone should go out there and set him straight. Or replace him. "

"And baptize the mermaid." Tadgh the friar sneered.

"But it hasn't been determined that she is actually human!" one of the others interjected in a worried way. "Wouldn't we have to send to Rome first for permission—or at the very least, the archbishropic at Tuam—for permission?"

"I don't think we need to bother Rome or Tuam with this matter yet." Fulke made little attempt to hide his distaste for the Church's bureaucracy. "I suppose a scholar should go and examine the matter in depth. I suppose, I should go myself. I seem to be the only one here who could look at the matter objectively and dispassionately, from the viewpoint of a canon lawyer. I must say, my curiosity has been raised."

"I will accompany you, my lord!" Aedan said quickly. Too quickly, earning curious stares from the teachers around him. He blushed. "After all, I was born there," he explained. "And I'm fluent in many languages, including the native Irish. Perhaps I could help in...communicating, with the creature."

Fulke gave him a small smile. "What language do you think a mermaid speaks, my boy?"

The others chuckled, and Aedan again turned pink. "I don't believe in mermaids. She is likely an ordinary woman. But I may help you to understand where she is from, and whether she has received God's good grace. Begging my lord's forgiveness, but you will not be able to make yourself understood on that island."

"That's the truth, sir," Paulus agreed heartily. "There's no one who'll be speaking the King's English, and they might run you off the island entirely. Best you take the boy, the local son, with you."

Fulke bit his lip thoughtfully. Like most Norman descendants who now dominated Galway city, Fulke, despite his education and piety, possessed an inbred distrust of the native Irish, regarding them as ruffians and primitive warriors.

"I see no harm in it," he replied. "As long as Aedan's interest in this creature is *purely* academic and spiritual in nature."

"Yes, m'lord." But Aeden felt somewhat ashamed, knowing his interest was neither academic nor spiritual, but sheer wanton curiosity. But nothing untoward could happen, he knew, in Lord Fulke's presence.

Aedan was also curious about something else, something he could not quite share with Lord Fulke: He felt a sentimental and irrational desire to see the island where he was born. He had never been to Inis Ghall and had only seen it as a crude irregular blackish dot on a hand-drawn map of Connemarra's coast. He wished he knew more about his mother and her family. He did not even know her name: Jacobo had never told him. The others said she had likely died in childbed. But who was she, and what sort of people did she come from?

Late, late that night, long after the midnight prayers, Aedan slipped into the library room. He thumbed the worn sheepskin pages of many ancient books, before finally coming upon the image he had remembered seeing: A tiny woodcut of a smiling woman with long wavy hair and bobble breasts, but below her belly button was a fish's tail, complete with carefully detailed scales. He read the Latin text alongside the picture: *A mare-woman found by the blessed Hibernian saint Brendan on his journeys, baptized and converted to Christ; through miraculous intercession, she was restored to human form and spent the rest of her days in a Breton nunnery.*

He took in a deep breath, surprised and delighted by this reference to his favorite saint and voyager. But at the same time, he could not quite believe it. Was his father right? Was Brendan himself nothing more than a myth, or merely a teller of tall tales? Doubt began seeping into his brain, a poisonous thing, the very thing Lord Fulke had warned him against. Too much thinking, too much rationalizing, he said, was dangerous to faith.

Perhaps I am *not* meant to be a priest: This frightening, breathtaking thought coursed swiftly through his mind, before he shook his head to dispel it.

The journey to Inis Ghall would be a good thing, he thought, a blessing. Away from St. Alban's, he would be able to think more clearly. And to see this girl...if a mermaid could truly exist, then so too could Brendan and his amazing voyage. Aedan would feel more confident about continuing into the vocation that Lord Fulke had chosen for him.

But if the lass turned out to be perfectly ordinary, a mere mortal...

Aedan sighed deeply, already seeing the hints of dawn piercing the thick leaded-glass window of the library. There was nothing else to do, he thought, but to go and see the lass for himself.

7.

Marra ran across the rocky stretch of gorse and dune as the sun began to rise, running back to her cave after a night of exploring. She ran and ran, not daring to glance back, hoping no one had seen her, or was following. She had to dodge the strange beasts that lived here in the isle's empty middle, animals with thick yellow-gray fur and dull, milky stares. They frightened her, these creatures, even though they barely moved and regarded her with a distinct lack of interest. She sped past them until the ground beneath her feet turned to sand and solid rock.

The cliff loomed high against the still-dark sea and sky, encircled by the raucous seabirds. She clambered up the big boulders and rock, to the hole at the cliff's top which opened to the sky. Having tired of the low damp ground-level cave Colm had left her in, she had investigated the others and chose this top-most entry, which seemed to her the biggest and most hospitable. It was cool and dry, with plenty of room to stand up and walk around. But the climb, which she could manage herself, was difficult enough to discourage most likely intruders.

Standing at the doorway, high on the cliff, overlooking the ocean and now looking down at the circling seabirds, she reflected on her life since coming ashore on this very strange island. For she had indeed *come* ashore, and had not been thrown up on it, by chance--by swimming away from her captors, in the cold dark seas of night, until stumbling in the surf and collapsing from the sheer effort of it all.

Every night, when the sun set, she went out to stealthily explore her new home, trying to understand what sort of place she had landed in. She still did not know if she were on a single island in the middle of the northern ocean, or if there were a great mainland nearby. But she knew for certain now this was not the land of her captors. These island people spoke their own language, more guttural and sharp. It sounded to her ears like grunting, at first, the utterings of beasts. As with her own people, she thought, there must be many tribes among the pale people, each different in their own way. Did they war and quarrel with each other, or trade peacefully? She still had much to learn.

But in her secret sojourns at night, she saw, to her horror, that the islanders seemed to be falling ill from the same sort of fever she'd had, and her captors had as well. Had *she* brought it to the island? Perhaps the boy Koe-lum had told them all about her. How she brought illness and death: They would likely try to kill her if they found her.

Should she stay here, or try to escape to another island or land? But where could she go?

51

She pulled Anhin's cloak about her, re-pinning it at the shoulder with a sharpened thorn, as she had seen other women of the island do. It was of woven wool, but tufted, felted, so it was quite warm despite the moth-holes and tattered edge. On her old island, they had no need of such garments; the sun was always bright, hot on their bare skin. She still could not get used to the feel of fabric, even after wearing the stiff linen shift for so long on the ship; she hated the feeling of fibers chafing against her skin. But Marra knew she had to wear it; she had to stay warm, in order to stay alive.

She gazed down at the seabirds, and knew she would be safe here. For some reason the islanders did not come here, nor did their strange yellow-gray beasts. She could see in the wan light of day that the caves were not completely natural formations; she understood they had been partially fashioned by men, for the walls facing the sea were carefully cut and stacked stone, her own doorway a perfect arch. It had been abandoned, perhaps centuries ago. A sacred place, maybe. But inside the cave, it was dark, cozy and deep within the interior, a hole in the ceiling allowed her to build a fire inside, so the smoke could escape. Hollows in the rock outside the entrance provided fresh water from rain, and below there were shellfish and plenty of sea-bird eggs to eat. She could rest and sleep without fear of someone coming upon her suddenly. But she missed the gently rocking hammock of her warm island home, the sound of the rustling palm-leafed roof of her father's hut. It seemed inhuman to sleep on cold, hard rock.

The journey across the great sea, across the world, had seemed endless. The first week had been so dreadful she could barely remember anymore: Her mind would not let her go back to that time.

Her father had been killed the day they were captured. The men aboard the ship--ugly, loud, pale dirty men--had grabbed at her hair and pawed at her naked skin, and her father, in a rage, had run at them, attacking them with his bare hands. It was Oo-roko, the ship's captain, who killed him with his long blade. Then he yanked the big pearl off her neck, without a word, and slipped it into his pocket. She was pushed into the dark, dank hold of the ship.

The first few weeks, she was kept tied up below deck, with the animals: A few giant turtles, still alive but stored stacked atop each other, and a few mangy goats. She understood. Unlike the wild Caribe tribes, who could be terribly cruel to their captives, but also human sometimes, taking the girls and women as their own wives, the pale men considered her *not* human, an animal to be caged with the others. But what would they do with her? Would they eat her, as the Caribe sometimes did with their captured enemies? She begged the *zemis* and sea gods to help her, spare her.

An old man in black garments came down each day with a bowl of fishy gruel for her to eat. He also forced clothing on her, the stiff linen shift covering her from shoulder to knees, and some kind of heavy garment which covered her arms and back. She did not try to remove them. It was chilly and damp in the hold, and the air seemed to be growing colder still, as if they were moving far away from her warm island. The man would stand over her, talking in a low tone, holding a square item, which she later learned was called a 'book.' But he never spoke directly to her, or even look at her ace, as if she were something rather unpleasant, or even frightening.

The days dragged by as the ship sailed on. The man who brought her food continued to come, but he seemed tired, weak, lethargic. One day he untied her and mumbled some words to her, then went away. Confused, she sat among the turtles and animals, waiting for his return, but he did not come back.

Some time later, she would come to understand he was the ship's shaman, or religious man, who was called 'priest.' And that he had died, shortly after untying and leaving her. She realized his presence had kept her somewhat safe, that he had kept the other men on the ship from ravaging or raping her.

Now she was on her own. Cautiously, she emerged onto the deck, blinking from the sudden shock of sky and sea. There were few men about and the air was quite cool now, the winds fierce and waves large and choppy. The men she did see stared at her with glazed eyes and dull expressions, and she suddenly understood: They were all *sick*, with some mysterious malady. A fever, she guessed, judging by the pink streaks on their pale faces.

She glanced at the sea. She could escape now, jump overboard and swim, but where to? These were foreign waters, cold and unfriendly: She knew to dive into them would be certain death. And she was not quite ready to die, yet.

The voyage grew yet more strange. The very earth itself , indeed the universe, seemed to change. The sun and its warmth disappeared as the sea grew rougher. The daylight grew shorter and shorter and the nights were frighteningly long. The air was so cold, like slivers of flint, colder than she ever believed could be possible. The ship, she sensed, was heading north, extreme north, into some kind of bitter underworld of cold.

The sick men put what was left of their energies into desperately keeping the ship afloat. They shouted and screamed to each other, and she crouched in the shadows, listening, trying to pick apart their strange words. She understood the tone of urgency in their voices. They were panicky, despairing, perhaps lost. They no longer knew where they were.

And where was Oo-roko, their leader? Sometimes she saw him approach, and hid from him. He was an ugly short man who frightened her with his yellowish face, scruffy hair and beard and rough voice. He seemed to be forever shouting and yelling at his men.

He also did not look good. He will be sick soon, she thought.

One night she struggled back up to the deck and saw a sight that made her joyful at first: Land! A great archipelago of strange, flat islands without color. But when she studied these isles closer, she saw they were not made of earth at all. They were solid, floating clouds without color, pure white tinged with the blue of sky and the coldness that blew off them nearly seared her face.

Izotz—ice—one of the sailors said, his voice leaden and lifeless. Frozen water.

Night fell and the sun did not rise again for some time. The ship creaked and shuddered and came to a stop. Caught in one of the heavy frozen clouds, it became trapped.

And there they remained. Oo-roko appeared from time to time, once to shout some curse at the skies, some invisible god up there. Then she did not see him at all for many days. Some of the surviving men managed to catch some fish—good-tasting fish, plump and gray with sweet white flesh. They no longer regarded her as an animal or beast, but treated her as one might treat an orphan or stray dog, throwing food in her direction but generally leaving her alone. Sometimes they caught one of the bigger black beasts called seal that lived among the floating clouds; she liked the chewy, fishy-meaty taste of these animals, even when it was not cooked. Chunks of the ice were melted for drinking water.

The ship groaned and creaked in its prison of ice, and she watched soberly as the men wept and cried and fought with each other. They ignored her. She continued to lay low, skulk about, learning their words. She was beginning to understand several words strung together, and thought she even understood some of their conversations.

Finally, the sun returned, briefly at first, then a little more each day. The ice began to give way and slowly released the ship from its grasp. The remaining crew set sail into open water again, in a straight easterly fashion. The air grew less icy and more benign.

On the night before she left the ship, she roamed about in the dark, searching for some kind of food, but instead coming upon the captain Oo-roko in his own room, lying abed, deathly pale, sweating under a great pile of woolens and furs.

She crept into the room and stared at him. He stared back up at her, his gray bloodshot eyes malevolent, but his body apparently unable to move. It was as if his body had died, but his head lived on. He blinked, but was unable to speak or curse or say anything to her. She saw his clothes lying nearby, calmly picked them up and searched through them until she found her pearl. Then standing before him, so he would see, she defiantly tied the pearl back around her neck, before leaving the cabin.

She hid away the entire next day, avoiding every man on the ship. That very evening at twilight, she saw it: A thin line of dark against the horizon, and the welcoming swirl of seabirds. She did not think twice, and clambered up over the side of the ship, letting herself drop into the coal-black ocean below.

Now her whole world was reduced to this cave, this cliff, this sea. It was immensely preferable to the rocking, creaking, claustrophobic confines of the ship; here, at least, she was completely free, under no man's rule. And here she would stay, until she understood what kind of people she had fallen in amongst. She would observe them closely and try to learn their words. She sensed they were a peaceful tribe, not like the evil-tempered sailors, but simple farmers and fishermen, much like her own people. Perhaps in time, she would join with them. Perhaps one of them would take her as a wife, though that idea rather disgusted her. They were so primitive, so...dirty!

Would she find a gentle pale man, one who would love her dark skin and eyes, one she could love in return? She wondered what sort of offspring they would have. Would they be pale, like their father, or bronze like her? Could she love a colorless babe, with white-sand hair and pale-sky eyes?

8.

The vicar of St. Alban's and his pupil Aedan set out for Inis Ghall on foot, making their way from the hilly districts of Galway through the web of tight alleyways, over the western bridge and beyond the city walls. They traveled west past Claddagh and its fishing *curraghs*, the Barna strand, past more stretches of sandy beach, seemingly empty lands, and then beyond. They encountered only the occasional farmer trotting his produce into Galway, or an old crone gathering driftwood and sea weeds by the shore. The bleak road was not profitable enough for robbers and highwaymen, who in any case feared the old Irish clansmen who ruled these lands more fiercely than any English soldiers.

The journey took most of a day. They had tried to time it with the tides, having been told the isle could only be reached on foot when the water was low. But the tide was quite high when they caught sight of the island across the strait. Not a single ferryman in sight: Fulke and his student were forced to sit on a beachfront boulder, and wait. Fulke unwrapped a Spartan repast prepared for them, a loaf of dark bread and a chunk of hard cheese and some dried currants. On the hill that loomed just above them, facing the island of Ghall, rose a huge, rectangular stone fortress, with tiny square windows squinting suspiciously out to sea.

"That is the castle of the local chieftain, I take it," Lord Fulke remarked.

"The fortress of the O hEynne," Aedan replied. "That's what Brother Paulus told me. That clan controls this stretch of coast and several islands, including Inis Ghall."

"I know that name," said Fulke, with some interest. "They are good Christians. I believe they endowed a convent and a small hospice within the city. I have not heard anything of them recently." He glanced up at the fortress, then turned his attention to the isle across the strait.

"The land of your birth. Not terribly impressive, is it?"

"No, m'lord." Aedan struggled to hide his disappointment. What had he expected, after all? A healthy, bustling city-island, with fine stone houses and church steeples? As Lord Fulke silently read his breviary, Aedan gazed beyond the shallow, lapping waves at the jumble of flattened trees and boulders. He did not see any hint of human habitation at all. He watched, as the afternoon sun waned and the tides did their work, slowly shrinking the expanse of water between the mainland and the island.

He found himself reflecting again on the matter with Jacobo. His father was now gone, well on his way to Madeira by now, though Aedan knew the journey would take several months, and only a few weeks had passed since his departure. If only he'd had the courage to go with him... He prayed his father would not be too disappointed with him. He hoped his father would have a safe trip; Jacobo was a man of many years now, and any sea journey could be his last, particularly one to a rather remote island in the Western Sea — indeed, at the very edge of the civilized world.

He did not ever expect to see Jacobo again, and this made him quite sad.

He glanced at the priest who had been his foster-father for nigh eighteen years now, worried he might somehow guess his thoughts. Sometimes he thought Fulke had that uncanny ability. Fulke's eyes were cast down on his book, but he did not seem to be actually reading. Feeling Aedan's eyes on him, he looked up, and gave him a rare, warm smile. The priest seemed oddly relaxed here in the out-of-doors, as if calmed by the breezes of the sea.

"How is it that you learned the forbidden Irish tongue?" he asked Aedan, but in a teasing way.

"Brother Paulus taught me. He is not from Ghall, but from the Saints' isles of Aran, further out in the bay, but he says the speech is similar."

"That Paulus is irascible. But a good man, a good brother. I am indebted to him for teaching you the dialect, otherwise I could not have made this journey. But I did not choose you for this journey because of your knowledge of the language. And I chose you in *spite* of the fact you were born here, and asked to come with me. "

"Why, then?"

"Because I believed you to be old enough, as well as mature enough to be a worthy traveling companion, like father and son. I think, at heart, you and I are very much alike."

"How, m'lord?" Aedan glanced back toward the island; a sandy path was just beginning to emerge from the lapping waves.

"In regard to many things. Your studiousness. Your seriousness. And, perhaps, in regard to more delicate matters...The female gender, for example. You do not seem to possess that irrational desire for women other young men seemed cursed with." He folded his arms together. "I should never have brought you here, if I thought your interest in this island girl was pure curiosity or wanton interest. I am not a hater of women; I respect holy women for their purity and intelligence. But I have never been troubled with that desire for them. I am not inflamed, preoccupied with these base matters of flesh. I am blessed indeed. As I suspect you are, as well, for you have never spoken to me of such matters."

Aedan was stunned. How had he done such a good job of hiding his intense curiosity about the other sex? As a child he barely knew women and girls existed, but recently...It was hard sometimes, to think of little else. He had noticed, on his brief journeys into the streets and markets of Galway, women and girls, young and older, fair and dark; he took notice of those who let their shifts slip past their shoulders or hitched their skirts to reveal shapely legs, and he had burned and ached with an unknowable, mysterious desire.

Lord Fulke was so impossibly wrong about him! Aedan did indeed envy the older man his calmness about such things, his holiness and cool purity. That, thought Aedan, is what makes him a great priest, a leader. *He* is blessed, but clearly, I am not.

Fulke laid a hand on his shoulder. "Look," he said. "The sea has parted for us, as it did in ancient times for Moses. It's time for us to venture forth."

They made their way onto the now-exposed floor of the sea, hitching up their long cloaks and weaving about the mucky puddles and mussel clumps. Aedan shivered as a long black eel slithered frantically across their path, but then he began to walk a little more quickly ahead of Lord Fulke. He was sure that something interesting awaited them on this island he'd been born on, perhaps some great adventure or revelation.

But when he actually set foot on the dry land of the isle itself, he felt intensely disappointed at the utter poverty of it. It seemed a filthy, primitive place of hovels and huts, stinking of rotting shellfish and seaweed. The few people who inhabited its tumbledown collection of shacks were dressed in tatters of wool; most of the children ran about naked, or nearly so.

Fulke's Norman nose quivered slightly, and his long lean face took on a pained look. "Best you were left with us at St. Alban's so long ago than to grow up here. Where do you suppose the island's priest is?"

They were directed to the church, a crumbling rock structure which seemed to meld in with the general chaos of the village. But there was a busy scene taking place there. Men and women were laying branches of driftwood and twigs and piles of hay alongside a large wooden stake, as if the islanders were preparing to burn a heretic.

"Where is your priest?" Aedan called out to them, in Irish. The stake-builders merely gaped at him and Lord Fulke, as if confounded by the richness of their garments. One ran toward the church.

Father Comgall emerged with the pale skin and red-eyes of a recent invalid, in a rough friar's robe of faded brown wool; his skin seemed to fall from his face, as if he had recently lost a great deal of weight. He regarded Fulke and Aedan with a blank look.

"Did they think I had died, the bishops? " He muttered, in Irish. "No need for replacement, I survived the fever, only just barely. It was a terrible thing, that illness, a ghastly thing —"

"Are *you* the priest of this island?" Fulke asked with both incredulity and disdain. He spoke in Latin, ignoring the other priest's crude Irish greeting.

"Yes, but could we speak in English? My Latin is terrible, but I still remember some of the English from my Galway days…Yes, I am Comgall, the pastor of this parish."

"Named after the saint who baptized a mermaid, according to folklore." Fulke drawled. "You seemed to be well named, my dear man."

"What?" Comgall gaped at him.

"You should know that old Irish tale," said Fulke stiffly. "The fisherman Beon who caught a mermaid in Lough Neagh, and brought it to his priest Comgall to be baptized."

"We've come to see *your* mermaid!" Aedan told him, perhaps too enthusiastically.

"There's no *murúch* here!" Comgall sputtered. "Only a malevolent dark spirit, who means to kill us all!" His eyes fell over Fulke's rich wool cloak and elegant robes. "We've had a terrible illness here, lord. Best you leave now, immediately before the tide goes out, save yourself and the boy."

Lord Fulke did not flinch. "We've come from Galway to investigate the matter of this so-called mermaid or witch."

"Did the bishops send you?"

"No, we are scholars of the Christian faith. Please tell us at once where this creature resides."

"I don't know! No one knows; she moves about. The islanders think she turns into a raven at daylight and flies away. Or perhaps a seal, or porpoise. She's only seen at night. But next time she ventures toward our homes, we will catch her. Then we'll burn her!"

"Burn her!" Aedan exclaimed. "Why?"

"Because she is *killing* us! She brought this terrible curse of fever to our island. It has killed more than half of us now. I nearly died of it myself and it killed my...housekeeper. My flock is dying. It won't end until we find her and destroy her." He suddenly squinted at Aedan.

"You're from Galway, you say? Not Saint Alban's, up on the hill there?"

"That very church," Fulke replied. "How do you know it?"

Comgall reached out to touch Aedan. "I...I know who you are, boy. I can see it now, in your

65

face and coloring. You are the bastard son of the girl Fiona! The yellow-haired lass who fell in with that Spaniard, in Galway. My housekeeper's own sister." And now his nervous expression turned to pleasure, at having recognized a long-lost island son.

"You knew my mother?" Aedan gasped in wonderment. He had never even heard her name before: Fiona.

"My housekeeper, Orlaith, was your aunt. Alas, she is dead of that wretched fever." He took Aedan by the arm more firmly now, in a conspiratorial way. "It was *I* who brought you to St. Alban's! Orlaith's father brought you to me when his girl Fiona died, he was a sick man himself, lame, a widower who could not work, and what could I do, a poor young priest? So I took you into Galway to find a good home for you. I chose the tiniest church in the city, a place that looked cozy, where you'd get a good upbringing and education. The priests at the cathedral, why, they'd probably have sold you off at the waterfront! It's good to see I chose wisely. You've grown up nicely."

"I am most grateful to you, sir."

The island priest continued to clutch Aedan's arm. "Talk to your old guy there, " he said now in Irish. "Get him out of here as soon as possible! I don't want the big Church getting involved in all this! Besides, the fever still rages. It's worse on the older ones."

"What does he say?" Fulke demanded in English.

Aedan turned to him. "He advises us to leave the island at once."

"Tell him we are not here to investigate him. I don't care if he is drinking the sacramental wine or how many illegitimate children he has running around here. We only need to see the female in question."

"I understand your English well enough," Comgall snapped. "It's for your own good I'm urging you to leave."

"But we need to see the girl with our own eyes," Aedan begged, in Irish.

Comgall grinned at him.

"I'm sure you would, my boy, though I don't believe her to be a comely lass. " He motioned toward Fulke. "This one strikes me as being not much interested in the fairer sex. Am I right?"

Flustered, Aedan began to blush. "If you could just tell us," he began, in English, "Where she might be now? Or has she left the isle, perhaps on one of the ebb tides?"

"Oh, she's not left. That we know. She continues to haunt us at night, like a furtive animal. Her work on this island is not done. I'm sure she cannot rest until we are all dead. If a wolf comes and kills your sheep, you kill the wolf, right? The people of Ghall are my sheep. I am determined to protect them from this evil sprite."

"Sprite?!" Fulke was nearly apoplectic. "My dear man, really! Men of the modern Church do not believe in such superstition. And in any case, you are not allowed to judge and wantonly kill someone you suspect of a crime, however

67

outlandish. She would need to be tried, first, by a credible judge."

"How can you try something that doesn't speak, or works witchcraft?"

"Nevertheless, that is not for you to decide. You would need to consult your superiors, the bishop at Tuam, and certainly the chieftain O hEynne who rules this isle. And it all seems moot, since the woman in question is not here, and perhaps never existed in the first place..."

Aedan was looking about the island and its people, feeling cheated and frustrated. No mermaid! He saw only wattled huts, poor villagers, boulders, mud and sheep. The island was mostly flat and nearly treeless—the needy islanders likely chopped them all down generations ago. Where could someone hide on such an island? He considered this for a moment, then came up with a plan. He did not think Lord Fulke would like it very much, however.

He took his teacher aside. "My lord, it seems to me that the only chance of witnessing this creature is at night."

"Surely you are not proposing we spend another moment on this wretched isle!"

"But if we leave, and there is such a person, the islanders will hunt her down and kill her without due process. That would be a huge sin."

Fulke sighed. "My dear boy. Isn't it clear to you that there is no mermaid, no witch? The hapless islanders have been struck with an illness they can't explain. So they developed this story to understand it all. Perhaps a whale strayed by, or an overly large seal. That would be the mermaid, the black witch from the sea."

"I can't agree, my lord. I think the priest speaks something of the truth. The creature he talks of surely is not supernatural. But she is in danger."

"Look, we must depart at once, before the tide comes back in. We will leave the islanders to their own madness."

"Please, sir. Indulge me just this once. This is where I was born. These are, as it were, my people. I don't feel danger for myself here. Let me stay and help them. Let me find out the truth."

"I will not allow it!"

"Just one night, and I promise in the morning to return straight away to the mainland and back to St. Alban's. You cannot forbid it," he said, gently, "For I am grown now, but have not taken any vows."

"I cannot allow it," said Fulke, in a softer tone. "Because you may catch the fever that rages here. We cannot lose you, Aedan."

"I will avoid the islanders and talk to no one. I will not sleep, but lie awake all night and wait for the witch to appear. If she does not, if she is indeed naught but fantasy, then I will return, chastened and humbled, to your walls."

"There are other dangers...danger. Females can be very dangerous to men in their own way."

Aedan flushed. "I don't know what you mean, sir."

"You know perfectly well what I mean! You are no longer a child, almost a man. While I believe you are much like myself, immune to the coarse charm of the female gender, women can be devious. All I know of them is what I've read or what other men have told me. But I understand that certain females can have a powerful effect on men, and lead them into temptation and ruin. A boy like yourself could be easily seduced."

"I will not be," said Aedan fearlessly. "I doubt any girl or woman could shake me from my studies."

"You may not be as strong as you think you are."

"I have no interest but to keep the islanders from doing violence to a possibly innocent human being. I could surely help her escape, couldn't I, or bring her to Galway for judgment?"

"Do your Christian duty, and no more. Do not lay so much as a finger on her, lest your soul be lost forever."

"I won't," said Aedan, earnestly. As mysterious and alluring as females could be, he could not imagine one getting the better of him. Especially some poor foreign wretch whose only crime was to wash ashore on the wrong isle. "I vow it, Lord Fulke. I shall come back to you as chaste and whole as I am now."

Fulke smiled weakly. "That is what I needed to hear. Very well, then. I don't like the idea at all. But you have been well reared and educated, I must trust your judgment. I cannot forbid you to stay, nor can I quench that adolescent desire of yours for adventure. So be it, Aedan. I will leave immediately to avoid the turning tide. Perhaps I can persuade the O hEynne to lend me a night in their manse before I return to the city. Let this night be your adventure. I daresay this mucky fog-bound isle will quell your adventurous spirit. When you return, I expect a stronger, wiser sort of young man, ready to take his vows and be of service to our Holy Mother Church."

Fulke left shortly after, with just a brief worried look back at his student before he set off across the strait. He just managed to make it across the sound, before the ocean swallowed up the path to the island.

Aedan watched him go with both regret and relief. He did not want Fulke to worry about him, but he was eager to begin his search for the mysterious dark maiden of Inis Ghall.

9.

Despite his promise to Lord Fulke to avoid other islanders, Aedan spent the early part of his evening with his "uncle," the island priest Comgall, and his family, sharing a simple dinner with him, boiled marrow-bones and withered root vegetables Aedan could not identify. Comgall gratefully accepted the half-loaf of dark bread Aedan had not consumed earlier that day, and ate it with great gusto, after giving a small portion to the small boy and girl who also shared the table.

"I cannot tell you the last time I tasted real bread," the priest said wistfully. "We never have it here. When we got oats from the mainland, Orlaith would make bannock-cakes. But true bread is quite a luxury."

Comgall's home was little more than a longish room, attached to the back of the church building; it had a thick oak table Comgall was quite proud of and a primitive stone hearth, with hay bunched in a corner for sleeping.

Though shocked at first to find a priest living openly with his own children, Aedan was pleased to meet his first cousins. Other than Jacobo, it was the first time he'd met someone actually related to himself. Little Itta, named for an ancient Irish saint, was a sweet lass of three, with a halo of tangled blonde curls. Aedan looked for his mother's face in hers, for Comgall said she greatly resembled her aunt Fiona. Colm seemed about ten years of age, his face a youthful version of Comgall's. He was short for his age, with bright red hair and freckles. But he seemed not much interested in his cousin from Galway; he ate silently and sullenly, his eyes cast down on the table.

"Colm here is an artist!" his father said heartily. "He'll be painting church ceilings on the mainland some day, I have no doubt." He rose to show Aedan a picture crudely painted on a plank of wood with clays and crushed charcoal. It seemed to be a battle scene from the ancient pagan days, startling in both its execution—full of detail and finely drawn for a boy his age, thought Aedan— and its copious use of the color red. Blood and severed limbs abounded.

"And here is another...I hadn't seen this one, Colm." He showed Aedan a sketch of a young woman's face, an unusual high-cheekboned face, with large dark eyes, framed in straight, jet-black hair. Colm hid his head in embarrassment.

Aedan studied the sketch. The girl, he thought, was quite fetching, but also very unusual. There seemed something foreign, almost alien, in her features, something that gave him a strange feeling in his stomach. He was both drawn to her, and little frightened as well.

"Is this an island girl?" he asked the boy, gently.

Comgall seemed alarmed. "Who *is* this girl, Colm? This is no island lass! Is she the one we're looking for?" he asked sharply.

"No," said Colm. "She's nobody."

"You imagined her."

"Yes." Colm would not look up.

Aedan said nothing; the girl's features seemed too interesting and detailed to be imagined. And he sensed the boy was hiding something from his father.

"I don't think the *murúch* or witch would be so winsome," he said, suddenly, to distract Comgall's sharp attention from his son. "Likely she would be a hag, with blue skin and seaweeds for hair, don't you think? Witches are never pretty, in fairy stories."

"There's nothing pretty about this miss who's running about, infecting us all. She is likely the daughter of Satan himself!"

"You know nothing about it!" Colm suddenly snapped. He leapt from the table and went to hide in the hay.

"Show respect for your parent, especially in front of the stranger from Galway! Even if he is your cousin." Then, in low whisper to Aedan. "I think he's actually seen the girl himself. He's not himself lately, so glum and secretive. I fear perhaps she's bewitched him."

"I haven't seen her!" Colm cried out from the corner.

"Is there anything else you can tell me about her?" Aedan asked Comgall.

"I don't think you should seek her out, my boy. It could be very dangerous. You are more than welcome to stay with us, but I wish you had listened to your teacher. This is not a good time to be on Inis Ghall, with the illness still going round. And this girl...well, if she exists, she could be dangerous."

"I don't believe in witches and spells, or anything supernatural. I would bring her to Galway to be converted!"

"That would be a pretty trick! If you could get her off the island without anyone murdering her...Or her, murdering you."

"Where would she hide during the day?"

"I'm not sure, but I imagine she might live in the pagan caves on the west end of the island. But you cannot go there."

"Why not?"

"It's forbidden!"

"By whom?"

Comgall was flabbergasted. "Why, by your own church and mine! 'Tis the place where the evil devil-worshippers of old conducted their rites. They sacrificed other humans there, in a barbarous way. Good Christians may not set foot on that part of the isle."

"But that was centuries ago!"

"The spirits and ghosts of the murdered live on there, and can infect any unwary traveler to that site."

"I cannot believe, my uncle Comgall, that you believe that!" Aedan was struggling not to be disrespectful to the older man, but he was astounded to find such superstitious beliefs in an educated, ordained priest, originally from Galway city! "I am not afraid of such things," he added.

"Well and good for you, then. You may head toward the west, just before sundown. You might catch her leaving her lair for the night. Stick close by the sea, that is where she fetches her meals, they say, eating like a fish or seal. " He leaned in close to Aedan. "I hate to see you go out there, but let me tell you this. Should you find her, forget this nonsense about bringing her to Galway! If she attacks you, *kill her at once.* Leave her body, so we might burn it. Do not give her the chance to practice her evil arts on you. I should not like to see Orlaith's nephew, Fiona's babe, killed or harmed." He paused. "Have you a weapon?"

"I won't need one," Aedan replied. "I won't be killing anyone. I will not lay a hand on her. I am only here to serve as witness and report to my superiors. It would be up to them, or the locals clans, to take action."

"Some islander may kill her first, although no one will go out to the caves. God be with you, my boy."

Aeden stepped outside into a cool spring evening, the sky just beginning to deepen from the setting sun. After so many years behind the walls of St. Alban's, Aedan realized he rarely took note of the passing seasons and weather. It was late March, and the Paschal season was nigh. Easter Sunday fell on April the 6th, lesss than two weeks away. Lord Fulke had been anxious to return to St. Alban's before the start of Holy Week, to celebrate the crucifixion and rising of the Lord Jesus. But here on Inis Ghall, it still felt like that bleak week that came after Christmastide. He could still smell winter in the air.

As he stared out across the island, he heard a yelp behind him. He was startled to see his small red-haired cousin running after him.

"Cousin Aedan, wait!" It seemed the boy had suddenly found his tongue. "I have to tell you the truth, before you find her. It was I who found her, washed up on the beach!"

"Found who?"

"The girl. It is a girl, a *cailín*, but with wonderfully strange features, and the blackest hair. At first I called her the raven-girl, but now I call her Marra, because she is from the sea."

"The girl in your picture? Why didn't you tell your father this?"

"He can't know! He forbade me to go to the pagans' caves. He'd *kill* me if he knew I was there! But I do go, all the time."

Aedan grinned. "And you live to tell of it!"

"It's not a dangerous place, just caves...but the girl, I don't know if she is good, or evil. I'm afraid perhaps she is some kind of witch. She looks like no other girl I have ever seen!" His eyes widened. "She was ill when I found her, and she made us all ill with that same fever. It killed my mother, and almost Father. But I think now it may not have been her fault. Why would she want to harm us, after all? We have done nothing, to anyone."

"So she is just an ordinary lass, then? From a shipwreck, do you think?"

77

"No, there were none this winter or spring. And she is far from ordinary." He dropped his voice. "She swims in the cold sea, with the fish and seals. I've seen her! And yet she runs faster than any mare or stallion, almost flying across the land." He paused. "You must go and see for yourself, cousin. But please, do not harm her or make her angry!"

"I'll take my chances with her. She lives in one of the caves, does she?"

"Walk straight through the sheep's field until you reach the open sea, then head west to the cliffs."

Aedan bundled his own voluminous green-wool cape about himself, as he wove his way though the flock of still-grazing sheep, trying to avoid soiling his fine leather shoes in the heaps of manure. He was dressed not in his student robes, but in a traveling-suit his father'd had made for him, a tight-fitting waistcoat of forest green over breeches of a lighter hue; a wide collar of snowy-white cambric spilled from his neckline, his long fair hair untethered and flying about. When he reached the strand, he thought the wind might knock him over. He walked faster to warm himself. The ocean roared at his side, the sky deepened to ultramarine and he felt his heart quickening. This was indeed an adventure! Not quite on the scale his father had promised, but he could not remember a time when he'd ever felt so bold, and *alive.*

After all, here he was walking alongside the great vast Western Sea, as it flowed into Galway Bay. This was the sea of Brendan and his navigators, Jacobo's sea, the ocean that held so many mysterious islands and secrets. The sea seemed to stretch forever without end, unceasing, yet filled with possibility…

He knew now he had made a great mistake in not going with his father. But it was too late now, nothing could be gained, dwelling on that.

As the sun settled on the horizon, staining the ocean pink and gold, he found himself approaching the island's lonely west end, a barren place of rock, gray limestone rising up into a cliff against the battering waves. Here he found small middens of empty shellfish and fish bones, along with a human's bare footprint in the sand. He bent slightly to touch the fresh impression: A narrow, smallish foot, perhaps that of a young girl. He then stared up, with some dismay, at the near-vertical face of the cliff. The sheer gray rock was rosy with the sunset and dotted with thousands of squat black-and-white puffins, birds he'd only seen as woodcut illustration in books. The air was nearly black with swirling, screaming clouds of gannets and gulls.

This was the 'pagan' temple? He squinted at the construction of rock, growing ever dimmer in the waning light. He had read descriptions of pagan structures—they apparently filled the Connemarra countryside, but were said to be simple constructions, usually one big stone balanced atop several others. Some skill had gone into these caves, he thought: There was some deliberate building involved, men had cut stone and carefully laid it, one by one. The openings were not cracks or gawping holes, but artfully constructed arches.

Aedan realized this was no pagan structure at all, but actually a very, very ancient sort of *Christian* holy place, perhaps dating from before the time of Saint Patrick himself. It was a place where the old-time monks and hermits went to be alone and pray, to remove themselves from the world. Aedan chuckled, at the islanders' ignorance. Pagans, indeed!

An interesting place for a witch or mermaid to take up residence, he thought. But he could see no hint or evidence of anyone actually living here, save for the piles of empty shells and bones.

He glanced at the last of the setting sun. He didn't have much time. He peered into a ground-level cave but saw nothing within. He decided to try and climb the cliff, to take a look at the biggest, and uppermost, cave.

But how?

He would never be able to scrabble up that vertical face, not without ropes or the help of other men. He decided he would try to approach from the backside of the cliff, which was more hill-like, less slippery and wet. From the summit, he would try to lower himself onto the ledge in front of the top arched opening.

But this proved no easy task, either. He found himself jumping, climbing from one enormous boulder to another, his palms scraped raw by the hard rock as he struggled to keep himself from falling backwards to certain death. The rocks were slick with bird dung. His cloak and garments seemed impediments, and his hair flapped into his eyes as he tried to see up into the night sky. The seabirds continued their nightmarish screams and cries, an assault on his ears. He was a scholar, a city lad—what was he doing trying to scale this mountain of rock?! Now he knew why Lord Fulke had warned him about excessive curiosity: It was dangerous!

But somehow he managed to reach the top, surveying a kingdom of night and sea-birds. *Dear Lord help me*, he prayed, just before beginning his descent onto the lower ledge before the top cave. *Don't let me fall and be shattered on this wretched rock. Don't let my life be taken from me, just as I am about to truly live.*

10.

Marra had been crouched down among the great boulders at the surf, searching for low-tide winkles and limpets, when she spotted the lone, pale young man in the distance, making his way toward the cliff-caves. Alarmed, she hid behind the largest boulder as the relentless waves assaulted her bare legs, watching him as he grew closer.

Who was he? What was he? Had he come to look for her?

She gripped the side of the rock and studied him closely as he neared. He seemed different than her captors, and much different still than the islanders. He seemed to be young, perhaps her own age, but he was as tall as a man. His cape was a vibrant shade of green, cut full and generously, lifting in the evening wind to reveal interesting clothes cut closely to his slender body. And those strange garments which covered his legs: Her captors had worn these, but the islanders, who wore only tunics and cloaks, did not. This boy had *shoes*, wrappings of leather that completely covered his feet. He must be wealthy and important, thought Marra, perhaps the son of a chief or some other important personage.

His cloak had been folded over his head to form a hood, but the wind kept undoing it. When it slipped away, she caught sight of his face, his magically fair hair—the color of gold! No beard—her people did not have beards or facial hair, so she liked this. His facial features were fine and handsome to her, his nose straight and long, even if the bones of his face seemed oddly flat to her.

But he was still a stranger; perhaps he'd come to catch and harm her. She could not let herself be enchanted by his looks or demeanor. She crouched lower. He carried no weapons, nor even a torch against the coming night. He came right up to the base of the cliff and gazed up wonderingly, with a boy's curiosity and confusion. Then he turned, and disappeared behind the cliff, perhaps to return back to the other side of the island.

She emerged slowly from her hiding place, feeling relief at his retreat. But also, a twinge of regret. He might have been different, this one. She had liked his garments, his fine face and golden hair. She made her way back up the front of the cliff-face as dusk was swiftly falling. She had become expert at this now and knew exactly where to place her feet. She was getting to know the rock, the cliff, as intimately as she had once known the tropical sea. She had gone from the world of pearl-oysters and coral to the world of sky and seabirds.

She set the shellfish she had gathered down by her improvised hearth and began to patiently coax the coals back to fiery life with small dry sticks. The cave seemed a lonelier place at night, when shadows danced on the darkened walls and nearly every sound made her jump. As she scraped the limpets from their shells, she became aware of some distant vibration, a scratching. She set down the limpets. It seemed to be coming from above. She glanced toward the arch of night sky, just as a small cascade of pebbles and gravel came raining down, clattering to the ledge below.

Holding her breath, she inched toward the entrance. She swallowed as a foot appeared from above—a foot in a leather shoe she recognized, as well as the corner of green wool. She lurched backwards, and suddenly, with a cry, the boy fell with a thud onto the ledge outside her door. He lay in a heap of wool, perilously close to the edge. He did not move.

She inched her way toward him. He'd hit his head in the fall and she could see blood glistening on his face in the moonlight. Common sense told her to kick him off the ledge, and be done with the threat he posed to her. He'd come here, no doubt, to get her, perhaps do her harm. But curiosity got the better of her. She dragged him by his feet into her cave, pulling him close to the fire, which now burned brightly.

Using a corner of her own cloak dipped in fresh water, she washed his head wound, which was not deep. But he had been knocked unconscious. As she suspected he was just a boy her own age. Seventeen, eighteen years...Almost a man, as she was almost a full-grown woman. She studied his face: She especially liked his nose, which was long and straight, and his slender chin. Wonderingly, she stroked his fair hair, so much like spun gold. Gingerly, she lifted one of his eyelids and was startled by the clear blue-green color of his eyes. It reminded her of the lagoon near her own island, the shallows just before the coral reef.

Perhaps he had not been hunting for her at all, she thought, but merely exploring as boys, young men, everywhere were wont to do. He was not of this island; She could tell from the difference in his clothing, which was finer and richer, and the style and cut of his hair. The island men had unkempt hair and beards, as had her captors, but this boy had taken some care to comb and shape his own, which fell neatly below his shoulders. Moreover, he was *clean*: He did not have the built-up filth and dirt on his skin or the lice she had seen on Colm and the old woman.

She took one of his hands in hers. It was smooth with long fingers and bony knuckles, not the hand of a laborer, farmer or fisherman. What did this boy *do*? Was he royal, the son of a king? But then why was he here, on this poor, rocky island? Perhaps he was too was a refuge like her, fleeing someone or something.

Would he be missed? Did he leave a mother and father out looking for him, a sweetheart perhaps? Somehow, she sensed he didn't have anyone, any family. She thought he might be a solitary boy, perhaps an orphan, alone in the world like herself. Otherwise, why was he out along on the strand at sunset, on the side of the island the others did not dare come to?

He slept on. She sat up with him, sleeping in a sitting-up position, and waiting through most of the next day. He seemed to be on the verge of awakening several times, only to lapse back into sleep. Toward evening, she saw a pink glow spreading across his face. The bleeding from his head wound had stopped, but he seemed very warm now — the fever! It came quickly, and burned fiercely, sometimes taking its victims to death within hours. She had to cool him. She gently pulled away the great cloak of green, pulled off his doublet, and something clattered out of a fold or pocket. She picked it up, and gasped.

"*Perla*," she murmured in astonishment, instantly recognizing the pearl-clam from her native waters. There were no such clams in this land! There were oysters and cockles and white flat clams that tasted similar, but their shells were lumpy, dull and not at all shiny or iridescent. No, this oyster was from *her* sea. Perhaps she herself had pulled it from the ocean bottom...

How did the boy get it? Who was he? Did he have some connection to those evil men who had taken her, and killed her father?

No, she thought: *He can't*. He is too fine, too gentle. She set the shell aside, vowing to forget about it. And then, because the boy was still warm with fever, she pulled off his white linen tunic, and stared at him. His skin was as pale as his face, his chest sprouting only a few golden hairs, his body slender, taut and smooth. She laid cool seaweeds and mosses on him, and in time, he seemed to be sleeping peacefully, in a normal way.

Night was descending yet again, and growing weary, she carefully lay beside him, throwing both Anhin's old cloak and his more voluminous one atop the both of them. After so many days alone, it was good to be with another human, even if he were still senseless, silent. But he was no danger to her now. She leaned toward him, grateful for the warmth, and fell asleep with good thoughts, believing this wounded boy had been sent to her from the gods, to relieve her loneliness.

11.

Aedan awoke to darkness. For an instant he could not remember anything: who he was or where he was. His head ached and he blinked desperately, trying to understand what had happened to him.

He was not at St. Alban's. He was on Inis Ghall. He had fallen off the cliff by the sea. He remembered that now. So why was he not dead or floating in the ocean? He was surely alive—the pain in his head told him so emphatically. He blinked again, and realized where he was.

Somehow he had gotten *inside* the cave.

How? And where was his shirt, his cloak, his doublet? He was wearing only his woolen breeches and linen under-breeches. He rubbed his head and tried to look around, but saw no one.

He sat up and endured a moment of vertigo, trying to focus on the opening of the cave. He dragged himself toward the hole of early morning light, his wool cloak around his bare shoulders and chest, then sat on the ledge, looking out. He found himself gazing out onto a cold gray dawn, a vast vista of ocean and a million cawing, shrieking birds.

And then he saw *her*.

She was standing on a ledge halfway up the cliff, about twenty feet down from him, fearless, oblivious to the dangerous position she was in. She climbed the cliff-face in a spider-like way, all the while carrying a clutch of puffin eggs in the lap of her shift.

She looked up: He saw the dark oval of face, high cheekbones and full lips, eyes like the night and black thick hair swirling about her in the sea winds. He opened his mouth to speak, to call out to her, but no sound emerged.

She continued to climb up toward him. He watched in astonishment at how easily she made her way up the rock. When she reached the mouth of the cave, she set the eggs down by the doorway and then, with the rough businesslike nudge of a mother cat tending its young, pushed him back into the cave.

"Who are you?" he whispered hoarsely, in Irish.

She ignored his question, instead bringing out other things she had tucked in her shift: A handful of live limpets, which she scooped from their shells with one finger and forced into his mouth. He nearly spit them out: Fresh shellfish was rarely eaten at St. Alban's, even on meatless days. Well-cooked mutton was the preferred dish there. But he chewed the snails gamely; they had a briny flavor that was not completely unpleasant. As she fed him, her sleek black hair brushed against his face, and he found himself marveling at her smooth, tanned skin.

Now she was tending a small fire toward the back of the cave, adding bits of straw and hay to make it blaze. She set the puffin's eggs right onto the fire and carefully removed them after their shells had charred. She then fed hard-boiled bits of the egg to Aedan, again with the determined seriousness of an mother bird or animal feeding her young. The eggs were egg-y like hen's eggs, but also fishy in taste. He nearly gagged and retched on them, but he continued to eat, not wanting to enrage or disappoint the dark girl-woman so determined to care for him.

She raised to his lips a clamshell, filled with cool, sweet fresh water. It tasted like wine to him, and he gratefully gulped it down. She gave him another, and another; each time she lifted her arm to bring the shell to his lips, her cloak opened and something caught his eye. Something glowing, shining…an ornament of some kind. Carefully, gently, he reached out, his fingers brushing her neck, the soft swell of her upper bosom. He felt something roundish and hard: a pearl, a *huge* pearl. He'd seen one once before, set into the silver cover of an antique breviary at St. Alban's. But that had been a scrawny, insect-like thing compared to this lusty stone, which was the size of a filbert, though with more of a pearish shape; and the color, too, of those late-season pears, a soft gold.

She brushed his fingers away, annoyed. He saw that he had acted stupidly, in touching the pearl — she must have thought he wanted to steal it. But the pearl intrigued him: it must be, he thought, a clue to her true identity. He remembered the pearl-shell Jacobo had given him. Where had it come from — India? Araby? Cathay?

He retreated to his resting place in the back of the cave, and studied her in the light of the fire, the angles of her face, the fullness of her lips, the fathomless depth of her eyes. There was something about her that reminded him of the female saints in old paintings and icons. She was no mermaid or sprite, but simply a foreign girl, a traveler who had come across the globe, across a great stretch of sea only to land, improbably, on Eire's primitive west coast. On Inis Ghall of all places!

He tried again to talk with her: In Latin, then English, French and Hebrew, which was the closest thing he could think of to the language of Cathay. He tried a halting inquiry in Spanish, one of his father's languages. She merely frowned in a puzzled way, and did not respond. He tried Irish again, talking slowly and emphatically. She regarded him with amused patience and utter silence.

Perhaps she was mute? He opened his mouth to speak again, but she firmly set a hand on his lips. She gently forced him to lie back, pantomiming sleep. He tried to obey, but his bruised head was swimming with curiosity. She was a puzzle he needed to put back together, but the clues seemed to be escaping him. He would understand it all, he thought, when he felt better.

But he suddenly bolted up again: He placed his hand on his chest and looked directly into her eyes.

"Aedan," he said, firmly. *"Eee-dunn,"* he repeated, thumping his chest for emphasis.

"Eeee-donnn," she murmured in response, seeming to understand. He then pointed at her, and she paused, as if trying to decide how to respond. She smiled, and placed her hand on her own chest.

"Mar-r-r-r-r-a."

He nodded, remembering that was what Colm called her: *mhara*, of the sea. That seemed an appropriate name for a girl who had emerged from the ocean. There was so much else he longed to ask her, but his head was throbbing woefully now. He needed to sleep.

And so in the lair of the sea maiden, he alternately slept and woke fitfully, obediently eating the fishy fare she force-fed him and gratefully drinking the water she brought him, clamshell by clamshell.

In his dreams, she shed her cloak and her legs turned to fish's scales before his eyes. Both Fulke and Jacobo came to rescue him from the cave, pulling him out like a snail from its shell. He dreamed that he and Marra shared a great carved and canopied bed and he awoke, to find her lying tight beside him in the cave beneath the blankets formed by their two cloaks.

She was sound asleep, though daylight shone in through the cave's hole. She was so close to him, he could feel her breathing, the beating of her heart. If he reached out, he could stroke the softness of her bronzed skin, lose his fingers in the thickness of her hair. Suddenly terrified, he rolled away from her, understanding at last, his mentor's words of warning.

He did not realize how strong desire could be. He realized he really did not know anything, about real life at all.

She awoke, and stared at him, puzzled.

"I—I'm sorry," he murmured, in English. "I wouldn't hurt you, Marra, not ever."

She merely smiled and went back to sleep. He felt shamed, foolish. What must she think of him? An idiot boy from the city, unable to care for himself, not knowing how to act with girls? He burrowed back under his cloak, and in a while, Marra left, presumably to look for more eggs and limpets. He found himself mourning her departure, the loss of warmth from their shared bedding place.

He slipped back into sleep. At times she woke him to make him eat. She brought the clamshells of the cool water he craved. At one point, as he was dozing, he felt her press the shell to his lips.

"*Urgeza*," she murmured, and half-consciously he repeated the word, Basque for water. The word lodged itself into his brain, but he was too sleepy to understand the significance of it.

And then she snuggled into the cave-bed beside him again. He felt a wild sort of joy feeling her beside him, so close, her raven hair glinting in the last coals of the fire, Oh Marra, he thought: *You have bewitched me already! What will I do?* He knew who could never hide his feelings from Lord Fulke, who seemed to read his mind and know everything about him.

Lord Fulke! The name filled his brain with sudden alarm. How many days had it been since they left Galway? And he was supposed to have gone back the very next day! How many days had he been here, in this cave with Marra? He could not even remember what day it was, and sometimes did not even know night from day. He did not even know whether it was still late March, or the beginning of April.

But it was night now, and somehow he managed to calm himself, and fall asleep again. When he awoke, he vowed, he would leave the cave, and he would surely return to Galway city straightaway. But for now he would spend just a few more hours in sleep with the warm and lovely sea girl by his side... It could not be so sinful, he thought, to merely sleep innocently side by side with a girl, no matter how beautiful she might be.

But suddenly, he was wrenched from his dreams, literally, being pulled from the cave to the sound of rough male shouts, in a language that seemed vaguely familiar to him. He was being yanked, dragged, and then, to his horror, he found himself dangling, with ropes tied about his waist, in brilliant daylight over the roaring ocean and careening seabirds, as several men from above hoisted him upwards.

Atop the cliff, a group of dirty, grizzled men, hooting at his bare-chestedness. His own linen tunic was thrown at him, and then the gang pushed him, barefoot, down the backside of the cliff.

He suddenly recognized their speech: Basque! *Marra!* he thought in alarm as he stumbled down the cliff, looking about wildly for her. She was nowhere in sight.

At the base of the cliff, a short barrel-chested gray-beard, dressed only slightly more grandly than the others, grabbed Aedan roughly by the neck of his shirt.

"Where is she, boy?" he demanded, in comically imperfect Irish. "Where is my girl? Where is my pearl!"

12.

Aedan stared in horror at the enraged bearded stranger who held him tightly by the scruff of his shirt. The man then pushed him toward the church and island settlement.

"March, you!" he commanded. "To the church!"

The man was a good head shorter than Aedan, but had the ferocious look of a wild, demented boar. Yellowish eyes, a dark beard mixed liberally with gray hairs and rotted, fang-like teeth.

"Who are you?" Aedan demanded of the man in Irish.

"Who am I? Who are you to be asking, boy?"

"I am Aedan de Adamo, a student at St. Alban's in Galway city. What do you want with me?"

"I told you what I want!" But the man paused. "*De Adamo*, you say? That's not Irish."

"My father was a Spaniard. Half Spanish, half Basque."

"You speak *Euskera*?" asked the man, in the Basque tongue.

"A little," Aedan answered, in kind.

"Ah!" cried the man with approval, slapping his back. "We're countrymen! I'm half Basque myself, half French. Look boy, just tell me where the girl is."

"What girl?"

"Please, no games. Urraco Vizkiero does not like games."

Aedan blinked, trying to summon a stray memory. Hadn't his father spoken of this man? Wasn't he the one with the bag of pearl shells?

"You were hiding out in that cave with her," Urraco went on. "Smooching it up with her or whatever. I know what boys your age are like. Only one thing on the brain, eh?!" He laughed raucously and slapped Aedan on the back again. Aedan, to his extreme annoyance, found himself turning hot and scarlet, his own red face betraying him.

"There was no girl," he said, stiffly.

"No, there wasn't. Not when we got there. Then what were you doing in that cave? Were *you* looking for her?"

Aedan glanced back toward the open sea, and now saw their ship moored just offshore, tattered yellow-brown sails fluttering, an unfamiliar flag. "I admit, I was looking for something. Someone. The villagers said there was a mermaid, I wanted to see it for myself."

Urraco laughed uproariously. "Of course you did! But she's no mermaid, just an ugly dark little thief! When I find her, I'll cut her throat. You can watch, if you like."

97

Aedan tried not to show his fear. "What did she take from you?" he asked, calmly. "Was it a pearl?"

"How do you know that?"

"You asked me! *Where is the pearl,* you asked, as soon as you saw me."

"Oh, there is no actual pearl," said Urraco, with affected casualness. "It is a...nickname, for the girl." He grunted. "Obviously, you know nothing. Boys your age are natural idiots, climbing all over kingdom come just for a look at a pretty pair of legs. Where are you staying? With the priest?"

"Father Comgall? Yes, I suppose, for now."

"Let's go and see what he knows."

Comgall was astounded not only to see Aedan again, but also the gaggle of strange and sinister men who accompanied him to the steps of the church.

"Aedan! Nephew, what has happened to you? Where is your coat, your cloak, your shoes? Who are these men?"

"It's a long tale, uncle. I fell on the cliff, hit my head..."

"Your teacher Lord Fulke has been wild with worry for you! He is on the mainland now with the chieftain O hEynne, trying to get a group of men together to search for you here. You've been gone four full days! Holy Week has begun, it's the first day of April!"

Aedan swallowed. "I had no idea."

"Why were you gone so long?"

"I hit my head. I blacked out." He paused. "You did not think to come and look for me, at the west end of the island?"

Comgall sobered. "No one wanted to go there. Not without the protection of O hEynne's soldiers. Listen, did you—"

"You were right, uncle," said Aedan loudly, so Urraco could hear. "There is no such thing as mermaids. Next time I will listen to you."

Comgall looked at him, then at the men, then at Aedan again.

"You have any drink, man?" Urraco demanded harshly in Irish. "Are there no inns or taverns on this hellhole island? How about some damned water? *Urgeza!*"

That word set off a firestorm in Aedan's brain. Marra had used it, in the cave. Did she speak their tongue? It never occurred to him, to try speaking *Basque* with her.

"All I have," said Comgall mournfully, "are some drams of stale ale, you'll have to be satisfied with that. I was saving it for Easter…"

Grunting, the men pushed themselves into Comgall's living space. The priest threw a desperate look at Aedan.

"Who are they?"

"They are mostly Basques," Aedan tried to explain. "Some French, some Spanish, some Portuguese…Fishermen, whalers, explorers." Then, in a whisper: "Pirates."

Comgall paled.

"Just give them what they want and hopefully they will be on their way."

Urraco gulped down the bitter, inky sediment-filled ale Comgall gave him and hurrumphed.

"It's swill! But it has a kick to it. More!"

Aedan waited until Urraco had downed a few more pints.

"My father tells me the Basque sailors are the bravest and most fearless of all," he said in *Euskera*, hoping he did not sound too obsequious. But Urraco was flattered; he smiled.

"Your father is correct."

"Where were you sailing from, before you came here?"

Urraco shook a stubby, warning finger in Aedan's face. "Never ask a Basque sailor that! We have our commercial secrets, after all. Why should the rest of the world know?"

"I only ask because at St. Alban's, I am a student of maps and geography."

"Hah! A strapping boy like yourself should be out on the sea. There's a fortune to be made these days, a huge world out there."

"So I've heard. Are you whalers?"

"We started out doing that. Too much damned hard work. Then we went after cod for a while. Boring! We've moved on to other commodities. For awhile we were sailing to the Ice-land, dealing in furs and northern ivory, bringing them down here to Ireland. That's how I picked up my bit of Irish." He quaffed down a few more ounces of ale. "Always had a soft spot for the land of *Patricio*, can't say why. But it's too damned cold here!"

"What do you trade in now? Spices?"

Urraco cast a contemptuous eye at him. "Hah! I see what you're getting at. We do not sail eastward. Who has time for that? That is for idiots, amateurs. Those Portuguese, inching their way down Africa's coast like scared little girls. I don't have time for that nonsense."

"You sailed *west*?" Aedan asked, boldly, and Urraco did not flinch.

"I'm not telling you if we did, or didn't."

"Which tells me maybe you did."

"Look, boy, you're annoying me! Where we sailed is my business and not yours. And not anyone else's."

"But I won't tell anyone. Who would I tell? I'm just a boy, as you say. A mere student. I'm not going to run off and steal your trade routes!"

Urraco did not answer. Aedan could tell he was fighting the urge to brag extravagantly.

"Where did this girl you keep talking about come from?" Aedan prodded. "The pearl? I bet there's a great story behind that!"

"You Irish love your stories," Urraco murmured. But the strong ale seemed to be taking affect on his tongue. His companions glared at him darkly, and one muttered something into Urraco's ear, but the older man waved him away impatiently. He pointed at Aedan.

"You want a story, I'll give you a story. Don't tell a soul, dimwit. It doesn't matter, since no one could match such a journey, not even another Basque. " He leaned in close toward Aedan. "We, my boy, conquered the Western Ocean!"

"Shut up *now*!" one of the other men growled, but Urraco slapped him.

"You shut up! Have respect for your captain and leader. " He sat back on the tree-trunk stool and began talking, in an odd mélange of Irish, Basque, French and Spanish:

"We set out first for the Canaries, intending to slide down the eastern coast of Africa a bit, just to scare up some easy capital—gold, silver, gems, real currency. But there was a good strong wind driving us westerly, so we decided to ride it out. We'd tried to go west once before, as far as we dared, only to be mired in the doldrums, stuck without wind in a sea choked with grasses and weeds. But this time fortune was with us—we made steady progress through good weather and gentle seas.

"But we had picked up a filthy fever in one of the African ports. They said it was brought in from Asia. Didn't seem to be any kind of big deal, but one by one, my men started to fall to it. It seemed to come and go, an annoying damned thing. I got it too, right at the end of our voyage. But I'm fine now. It was-- "

"You left Africa, and then..." Aedan prompted, trying to get him back on track.

"We continued to head west. I had a feeling something was lying out there, some great sort of land, full of riches, gold." His eyes glinted.

"The Indies?" Aedan asked. "The other side of the world?"

"Shut up and listen to my story. We hit that damned giant patch of seaweed again. It was hot as blazes, Hell itself. But then the wind started up again. I swear, it was like the hand of the Almighty Himself pushing us across that west ocean.

"And then, we saw them: Islands. Hundreds of them. Lush, green, full of the palms you see on the Mediterranean and in Araby. And the water, the color of it! You have no words in Irish to describe it. It's not quite green, not quite blue...why, it is the color of your own eyes, my boy! And filled with the most amazing sorts of plants and animals and creatures, fish by the netloads."

"Sounds like Paradise," Aedan murmured.

"On the shore, and in the shallows, we saw thousands of people, all dark-skinned and black-haired and completely, utterly naked, except for these fabulous gold ornaments they wore in their ears, their noses, every opening. They seemed quite excited to see us, so we rounded up our trade goods, glass beads from Venice, silk-cloth and what-not, and they rowed out to greet us, cheering."

Aedan, who was beginning to become mesmerized by this tale, suddenly glanced at one of the men, the one Urraco had slapped. He was rolling his eyes.

"They were astounded at our appearance, our very clothes," Urraco went on. "They immediately fell to the ground, and began to worship us, like gods! They took us to their chief, an old man, also naked but wearing a great peaked hat of solid gold. We waited for them to bring out more gold and jewels for trade, but first they arranged some sort of feast. A great table was laid out with fruits and vegetables such as we had never seen, roasted fowl and fish of every variety. There were bowls of a curiously strong spirit. When they drank this, they began to dance crazily, as if they were being stung by bees. They continued to dance and dance, into the night.

"Then suddenly, this *girl* appears. The daughter of the old chief, I'm thinking, or perhaps his youngest wife. She was a big, tall, proud, haughty beauty, dark as night, and around her neck she wore the biggest pearl ever created by an oyster. I tell you, it was the size of a man's fist and the color of a glowing fireball. We decided then and there to take both her, and the pearl, back home with us."

Aedan said nothing. As he suspected, Urraco was either lying or stretching the truth. Marra was not tall nor haughty, and her pearl was considerably smaller, too; it did not glow as extravagantly as Urraco claimed. And did he really expect Aedan to believe noble savages would fall down and worship a smelly ragamuffin gang of grizzled European fishermen? There *might* be a grain of truth in this story, thought Aedan: But where is it?

The now-drunken Urraco continued: "Well, we waited until dark to take her, since we suspected her old man would be none too happy. But we did not expect her to put up such a fight! She was vicious, like an animal! One of my men grabbed her about the waist, and she...slices his head off, right there! Kills him on the spot, along with two other of my men."

Aedan stared at him, dolefully.

"That's not the worst part, my boy. Her tribe comes forward, takes the headless body, and roasts it over a spit! And the girl herself plucks out the cooked heart, and eats it herself!"

"I don't believe it," Aedan snapped. Comgall grabbed his arm.

"What's he saying? I can barely understand a word of it!"

"He says he encountered some cannibals. And a dark-haired girl was one of them."

Comgall paled. "People who eat...other people? And one of them here, on Inis Ghall?!"

"He is lying," Aedan told him, but the story did trouble him. What if Urraco wasn't lying, about *that*?

"Not even the O Flaithertaigh could be so craven as that!" Comgall murmured, referring to a Connemarra clan known for their bloodlust. Urraco continued:

"Now the savages were all about us, and we had to fight them off as best we could. Our knives and swords were superior to their weapons, of course, and we killed a great many of them. Including the old chief, and I killed him myself, my own blade across his neck. I took the girl and her pearl with me; I wanted to make her pay for her evil act. I was planning to sell her in one of the big slave markets, for I knew her exotically strange appearance might command a big price and I knew the pearl would fetch a bigger price in the markets of Lisbon or Venice. "

"So why then did you come to Ireland, of all places?"

"Well, we didn't intend to, boy! This was the *last* place we wanted to come! But the weather and sea turned on us, as we sailed east again and north. I forgot it was winter up here. We were blown all the way north, almost to the Ice-land, and I thought, as long as we're this far, we may as well pull in at Galway...Not that I was planning to sell the pearl or girl here, you Irish are too damned poor to offer any real money. "

"Although, you were able to sell your pearl-oyster shells in Galway port, weren't you?" Aedan remarked, coolly.

Urraco's eyes narrowed. "What oyster shells?"

"The pearl shells you took from those western people. Whoever they were. You sold them to my *father*, Jacobo de Adamo."

"Oh-h-h-h, that Adamo! Huh! Cheap bastard, they were worth three times as much as he gave me. And not a single pearl in the bunch!"

"What?" Aedan feigned surprise. "No other riches? Why did you not take all that fabulous gold from the savages you slew? The people who worshipped you? What happened to the chief's solid gold hat?"

Urraco gave him a venomous look, but said nothing.

"Your story is completely false," Aedan continued. "The ravings of a drunk man! Is any of it true?"

"You wanted a story, damn you. I gave you one." He grabbed Aedan again by the neck of his shirt and nearly pulled him across Comgall's oak table. "This is true: There is a girl, a savage black-haired female. There is a pearl, worth a king's ransom. She escaped us somehow just as we came into this bay, just as we were passing this isle, and I am determined to find them both, even if I have to kill everyone else on this god-forsaken island!" And with that, he suddenly released Aedan from his grip, and passed out cold, head-first, onto the table.

"*Zozo*—idiot!" one of the other men snapped. He and the other companion heaved their captain onto the pile of sleeping-hay in the corner, then took their places beside him, one on each side. Soon, all were snoring loudly.

Comgall was appalled. "Must I keep these wretches here all night?"

"Let them be for now," said Aedan. "They are in no danger to anyone now, in the state they're in. It's the others, roaming about the island, I am more concerned with. I must think...I have to find some way, to deal with them."

"*Deal* with them! These are the worst kind of men! Are you insane? You should go back now to the city, to your church, your teachers. Your Lord Fulke will return in the morning with the O hEynne men. Let those fellows deal with the pirates." He looked Aedan in the eye. "You cannot save the girl."

Aedan stared at him. "But I told you, there was no---"

"I know what you told me." He sighed. "I know the truth. My boy Colm, he confessed everything to me, after you went missing. He looked for you and found you, asleep in the pagan cave with the dark girl he'd sketched on the board. " He shook his head. "Telling falsehoods, consorting with strange females in a pagan's cave...what would your Lord Fulke say?"

"My falsehoods were mild and I have done no other wrong." Aedan argued. "The girl, she is no witch, uncle, but a gentle maiden from a foreign land. She means no harm, but wants only to survive. We cannot let her fall back into the hands of the pirates."

"Seems she's bewitched you as well. Tell me, boy, what would you do with the girl if you found her again?"

"I...don't know. We would have to take her away, I suppose. Lord Fulke and myself."

"Where to?"

Aedan shrugged helplessly. "To Galway, maybe. We could try to find her people...There are many foreigners there."

"Likely not like her. She may come from a land yet to be discovered."

Aedan considered this. "We could take her to a nunnery or girl's school, where she would be safe—"

"And would you then go and visit her, in secret?"

Aedan blushed to the roots of his hair. Comgall grinned.

"There's the heart of it! You *do* have feelings for her. It would not be so wrong for you to love her— *if* she were an ordinary lass. But she is a danger to you and all of us, because of her association with these evil men, these pirates. If you take her away, they will come after you, maybe kill you both."

Aedan made no reply; he was full of confusion and regret.

"When my teacher arrives," he said softly, "Please do not mention any of this to him."

"Oh, he'll want to be knowing. You can't keep it from him. You'll have to confess."

"I'm confessing to you, aren't I?"

"He's going to know something's up. You two seemed close. "

"Yes," Aedan murmured. "We *were...*"

"And then you'll return to your studies, to Galway, as if nothing had happened. With, or without the girl?"

Aedan sighed. "I need to think on it all. Perhaps the answers will come to me as I sleep, before my Lord Fulke returns."

They settled down to sleep in the nave of the small church with the children, leaving the snoring foreigners in the room behind the church. Comgall, despite his determination to keep an eye on Aedan, instantly fell into slumber; but Aedan lay awake, sleepless, sandwiched between his two small cousins.

He could think of nothing and no one but Marra. The other men from the Basque ship were out there, in the dark, looking for her. He had no idea where she was, or how she might be eluding them. Perhaps they had already found her and — he couldn't bear to think of it. Filthy swine! He thought: I'd like to put a sword to them myself!

What had happened to him on this isle of Ghall? He had turned from gentle student to full-blown old-time Irish warrior! Was it something in the water, the wind, that made him want to go out and fight? He rose, and walked to the back door of the church, not intending to leave but merely look up at the stars and moon. The settlement was silent, the air crisp with cold, but suddenly he detected some movement in the leafless bushes that surrounded the back of the church. A shadow, a ghost...

He opened his mouth to speak her name, but she swiftly put a hand to his lips, then embraced him tightly.

"Aedan!" she whispered, fiercely happy.

He too felt himself rejoicing at her embrace. She pressed her face against his, and then her mouth against his cheek—he felt startled, remembering Urraco's story about the cannibals. But no, those were falsehoods. This was no bite, only a sign of warmth and affection. He gently stepped back, holding her by the shoulders.

"Marra. Where are you from?" he asked in the tongue of the Basques. His knowledge of his father's language was far from perfect, but he knew enough to communicate. "What land?"

She stared at him in surprise, but made no answer.

"I know you know some Basque," he continued. "Your land is where?"

"Across great ocean," she replied, her voice sweet, girlish. "Where sun go down."

"West!" he whispered, fiercely. "How far?"

"Very, very far. Many months, on sea."

"A cold place? Iceland, Greenland...Cold? Ice, at your home?"

"No. Is hot. Color, much color. Birds, flower. Fruit."

"What is the name of your place?"

She replied with a sound — *Loo-cah-oo* or *Yoooo-can-oo*, and he struggled to understand. "Island," she tried to explain. "Many islands. No big land, like here."

"Is it...the Indies? Cathay or Cipango?"

She looked confused.

"It does not matter now. Marra, you must leave this island."

"No," she said, emphatically shaking her head. "Not leave. Stay."

"*No!* The men, from the ship...they will kill you. They want the pearl."

She regarded him with faint suspicion. "How you know their words?"

"My father is part Basque. Not me! I am Irish. *Eiranach.*" He pointed to the ground. "My mother's land. "

She nodded slowly, as if understanding. Did she? he wondered, but he could see a real intelligence in her eyes. She must be quite smart, he thought, to learn the convoluted ancient tongue of the Basques.

"Don't you fear the sailors, your captors?"

She made a face of disgust. "Not scare me. They are stupid, *zozos* --I hide. They not find."

"But the island people here — they fear you, too. They think...you have made them ill with fever."

She grew serious now and said nothing.

"They may want to hurt you, too. No one can find you, Marra."

"I hide from all. In rock and sea. I never stop, always looking, hide. I have *house* now. Safe." She stepped back from him, and formally handed him a largish piece of wool cloth. Puzzled, he accepted it: It was a disgusting thing, reeking of stale fish.

"Eels. Man," she said suddenly. "House," she added, before slipping off into the night again. He did not call after her, lest he wake Comgall or the pirates.

But Colm suddenly emerged from the church, rubbing his eyes. He blinked at the gray cloth Aedan was still holding.

"What are you doing," he asked, "with old dead Donnacha's cloak?"

"The girl Marra gave it to me."

The little boy nodded. "That's a good place for her to hide. His hut is empty and cursed, no one will want to look for her there."

In the morning, Aedan awoke, to find Lord Fulke standing over him, silhouetted against the morning sun streaming in through the church's glass-less windows. The memory of Marra was still lodged in his brain, like a dream. The worn gray cloak of Donnacha lay off to the side, in a crumpled heap.

"What has happened to you, my boy?" Fulke's voice was barely a whisper, yet still full of sternness, anger, and relief. "Where in God's holy name have you been these past several days?"

Abashed, Aedan scrambled to his feet, and showed him the wound on his head. "Forgive me,

Lord Fulke. I never meant to cause you such worry."

"I knew leaving you here was a grave mistake on my part! Come, we are leaving at once."

Comgall now stirred, regarding Fulke with some alarm.

"Where are the Irish soldiers of O hEynne?" Aedan asked Fulke. "Did they not come back with you?"

Fulke shook his head. "They would not. They don't think there is any real problem here."

"What?! Didn't they see the ship anchored just off Ghall? Don't they know their island is overrun with Basque and Spanish pirates?!" Aedan was incredulous.

"Pirates!" Fulke paled. "And they've invaded this island?"

"Yes! They are swarming this isle as we speak."

"Then all the more reason for us to leave immediately. The tide is growing low. *Now*, Aedan."

Comgall now put his hand on Aedan's shoulder. "Go, nephew. You must return now to your studies, there is nothing else you can do." He added, in Irish: "You must forget the dark lass, there is no future in her for you."

"But I hate to leave you, uncle, and the island in such peril!"

"What can *you* do about it, boy?" said Comgall, gently. "The Great Lord himself will decide our fate. Go with your teacher, and keep us in your prayers."

Aedan felt utterly heartbroken. He had found what he came to discover, and the discovery was more astounding than he could ever have guessed it would be. A lovely girl from the far side of the mysterious Western Sea. How could he abandon her now, when she was in such danger? And yet, he could not defy his teacher and foster father, Lord Fulke.

"I will go with you now," he said, haltingly, to Fulke. "But I will return—"

"You will *never* return to this forsaken place!" Lord Fulke thundered. "And once we reach the gates of St. Alban's, I will never let you stray beyond the church gates ever again!"

Aedan was aghast. Could Lord Fulke do such a thing? Literally imprison him behind church walls? But he did not have any time to argue the point, for as soon as they emerged from the church door, one of the Spanish sailors surged forward and grabbed Aedan by the shoulders. The other began to tie him up in twine.

"What are you doing?" Fulke shouted. "This is my student, untie him at once!"

"Murderer!" the sailor shouted at Aedan, in Spanish. Horrified, Aedan glanced at his teacher.

"I have killed no one! " he cried in English, and Fulke gasped.

"We will awaken your memory," said the other sailor, pushing him into the room behind the church.

On the floor in the hay, the three Basque sailors lay sprawled out as they had the night before, seemingly still in a drunken stupor. Aedan, his hands bound behind his back, stepped closer to the men, to get a better look at Urraco in the middle. His linen tunic and waistcoat were ominously splashed with a dark stain.

Turning pale, Aedan glanced at his teacher.

"The pirate captain, Urraco. His throat's been cut! He's dead."

13.

Zachario, the Spanish-born sailor who had taken over as captain of Urraco Vizkiero's vessel, chuckled now with strange glee as he regarded the dead body of his former superior.

"You did us a favor, boy, by killing this fool. He was a lying, thieving, dangerous idiot. Half the time, he had no idea where we were sailing to. He exposed us to that damned fever in Africa. And he nearly killed us all on an iceberg in the far north. He needed to be dead."

"But I did not kill him!" Aedan exclaimed. "I have no knife, no weapons. I am only a student!"

Zachario looked at him casually for a moment, then shrugged. "All right. Cut him free, boys."

"What?!" the other sailors were outraged.

"He's right. *He* did not kill Vizkiero. But it was fun to throw a scare into the boy, wasn't it? Are your breeches still dry, little one?" He smirked at Aedan.

"Then who killed him?" Aedan demanded. "One of you?"

"No," Zachario replied, coolly. "Sorry to tell you this, but it was your dark-haired sweetheart."

"No," Aedan snapped, without thinking. "She would never have done something like that!"

Zachario chuckled. "You are so naïve, my boy. So innocent. You know nothing of women, do you? They can be cruel, crueler than men. And she was more animal than human. I would see the way she looked at old Urraco, with darkness in her eyes."

"He murdered her father, and stole her from her land."

"Yes, so she had reason then, didn't she? No matter. She has murdered our captain. She has stolen the only true thing of value we were able to collect on our last, miserable voyage."

"I thought Urraco said the western islands were filled with gold."

"And you believed him! You are a pathetic little boy. We found nothing, but a poor pearl-fisher and his daughter, in a leaky dug-out canoe. The only thing of value was around that girl's neck." He stepped back and now addressed Aedan—in perfect English, obviously for Lord Fulke's sake:

"You spent three nights lying in a cave with that brown female savage. Why don't you stay, and we'll see if the murderess comes looking for her lover."

Lord Fulke looked as if he might faint. "Is...is this *true*, Aedan?"

Aedan did not answer right right away, but once again his face betrayed him, turning a deep pink.

"Yes, there was a girl...But I promise you, m'lord, nothing happened between us! But simple sleep."

Zachario roared with laughter. "Either the boy is lying…or a eunuch!"

"We must leave at once then," said Fulke, with a cracking in his voice. "It is clear to me that your soul is in mortal danger. The only repair can come at home, in your studies and at the church. Come, the tide is still low, we must go now."

"But I have no shoes!" Aedan cried. "Or my cloak! I left them at the cave! I cannot make that journey with bare feet!"

"You can, and you will," Fulke snapped. "It will be the beginning of your penance, for whatever transpired on this unholy island."

Aedan cast one last, quick, regretful look about the island of Inis Ghall. It was not a pretty place, rather bleak and melancholy, but it had somehow become a part of him, imbedded in his mind and heart. Father Comgall and his cousins watched him mournfully as he made his way down to the eastern edge of the isle, shoeless and cloak-less, then onto the muddy path through the strait to the mainland, slowly, reluctantly following his Lord Fulke at a distance of about ten paces.

The return walk to Galway was quite long, and painful: the undersides of Aedan's tender feet burned as if he were walking on coals; he shivered in the shore winds, sorely missing his cloak. It was silent, too; Lord Fulke would not speak to his charge, who continued to walk some distance behind him. Something had broken between the two of them. Aedan knew his mentor and teacher, his erstwhile father, would never again trust him completely.

Aedan knew he should be contrite, penitent, begging Fulke for his forgiveness. But somehow, he did not *want* to. He felt he had done nothing wrong. And he was angered at having been forced to leave Inis Ghall, when so many questions still remained about Marra and her origins. What strange land had she come from? Who were her people? Had she murdered Urraco? She was likely not a baptized Christian, so perhaps she did not see it as a bad act. But didn't all civilized people see murder as something unacceptable?

And those idiot O hEynne, he thought with extreme annoyance, why hadn't they come forth to defend the island they ruled and owned? They might have prevented Urraco's murder.

He could only hope that Marra stayed hidden away, and would not be caught again. He wished he could forget all about her, and continue with his studies.

But he knew he could not. The memory of her remained strong, indelible, within him. He actually felt as if a hole had formed in his heart, an aching emptiness he had no words for.

As they approached the gates of St. Alban's — Aedan's feet were completely without feeling now — the priest turned to his student.

"You had feelings for this girl?" he asked.

"I cannot lie to you, m'lord. I wish I could say I didn't, but I did. She was quite extraordinary. She was the first girl...I ever met." He paused. "It's not a sin to *love*, is it, my lord?"

"No," Fulke answered quietly. "Not if you keep it secret, in your mind and heart. You say nothing serious transgressed between the two of you, physically?"

"I give you my word, lord. I am still as chaste in body as I was when I left these walls."

"Well, then." Fulke's demeanor seemed to soften. "Perhaps all is not lost. With a great deal of prayer and mental work, this unfortunate incident will soon be behind us." Obviously fatigued, the priest rubbed his forehead and sighed.

"This journey has exhausted me. I fear I shall have to retire at once if I am to have any strength for the morrow's Mass. You are to retire yourself immediately as well and recoup your own strength. But you are to be in the chapel before sunrise."

Aedan watched as his teacher walked down the corridor to his own cell. Fulke now walked with some difficulty; the journey had indeed taken its toll. But Aedan did not retreat to his own little cell. He went instead right to the chapel to pray, kneeling on the hard limestone floor; but all he could think about was the girl Marra. Her dark eyes and oval face floated before him.

He had abandoned her, left her to be murdered by the Basque pirates just as he had abandoned his own father Jacobo, by refusing to join him at sea. What sort of coward was he? Was he becoming a man, or would he always be a weak boy, of no real use to anyone?

I should have stayed behind. To help you, Marra.

But she was pagan, not Christian. What if she killed Urraco?

He bowed his head low. "Help me to understand, Almighty Lord. But keep her safe, from the pirates."

The islanders, they distrusted and feared her as well. He remembered with a chill, the stake they had set up, in front of the church.

Help me, Lord: I must pray to You and not think of the world beyond these walls.

How could he have left her there alone, defenseless, facing certain death, when she had perhaps saved his life, cared for him when he fell? And he had finally learned how to communicate with her! What else might she have told him of the world beyond the Western Sea, of a land Europe did not yet know of?

Why had he let Lord Fulke pull him away?

I must stay here, and continue my studies. Devote myself to Lord God and the Church. I must not disappoint my teacher and foster-father Lord Fulke again. I must not abandon him.

And yet, within the hour, he already knew what he must do.

He went to his cell and composed a long letter to Lord Fulke, a full confession of what had occurred on Inis Ghall, in the cave with Marra, his feelings for her and even Jacobo's attempt to lure him from the abbey. He wrote of his sorrow in leaving St. Alban's and Lord Fulke, but concluded:

I know my future and destiny is uncertain, but I feel unmistakably that it is God's will that I return to my native island and resolve the situation with the pirates and the foreign girl. I will never forget your kindness to me and I will be forever grateful for my education, which

121

I am sure will serve me well no matter what path my life takes from this moment on.

He signed it, *your loving son, Aedan.*

He slipped away from St. Alban's at dawn, taking with him only another cloak of undyed wool, another set of shoes and a loaf of bread from the kitchen. As soon as the city gates opened for the day, he left Galway city and made his way back along the sea-road, the same journey he had just made the day before, but in reverse. His heart was filled with mixed emotions, but the long trek calmed him. His pace quickened as soon as he caught sight of Inis Ghall in the distance. The Basques' ship still lay anchored off the western end. He felt he had made the right decision.

14.

Brother Paulus found the letter Aedan wrote to Lord Fulke, just where the boy had left it, on his neatly arranged sleeping cot. He read it, but did not give it to his superior.

For during the night, Fulke had become quite ill, burning with fever. He did not leave his bed the entire next day, and by day's end had slipped into a coma, barely breathing. Physicians were brought in to treat him, applying leeches and administering strong potions and medicines, but nothing would revive the vicar. He was given Last Rites, and was not expected to survive until Easter Sunday, only a few days away.

But on the morning of Good Friday, Fulke emerged from his unconsciousness with waxen face and sunken eyes. It seemed as if the fever had consumed his very flesh; always a thin man, Fulke now appeared almost skeletal. But he asked for water and bread, and the other priests and brothers took joy in his reawakening. It seemed a Paschal week miracle, coming as it did just before Easter Sunday.

But very soon it became apparent that the vicar of St. Alban's had undergone a profound change.

123

Gone was his quick intelligence, the mild sense of humor and gentle, if discreet, sense of superiority. Gone, too, was his piety, perhaps his faith as well. This new Fulke was now a frail, frightened, angry and bitter sort of man, given to startling, blasphemous oaths and irrational rants. It was as if, Brother Paulus noted sadly, the disease had eaten away parts of his brain and soul, changing the man forever.

"Our boy Aedan has left us, and our poor Lord Fulke has gone mad. 'Tis the work of Satan," Paulus declared in a dark tone to the others. "It's the curse of Inis Ghall. The island of foreigners — it has always been a sad, mad, evil place!"

But he did not reveal the contents of Aedan's letter, which he burned. And so the other brothers and priests of St. Alban's did not know what to think. They could only imagine what had happened on the small island in outer Connemarra, and to the young charge who had lived among them for so many years.

They kept their superior in a small cell off the infirmary and tried to calm him with sedating herbs and teas. They tried to keep all visitors away, but one imposing, middle-aged foreigner came stomping in the morning of Holy Saturday, demanding to see the man he claimed was 'imprisoning' his son.

Jacobo De Adamo now stood over the priest Fulke. He considered the priest, his son's foster-father, an odd, bookish sort of man who had always been formal and distant, never warm to

Jacobo. A secret rivalry or silent war had always existed between the men: their prize, Aedan.

"Where is he?" Jacobo demanded. "Where is my son!"

Fulke stared up at the Spaniard, his eyes watery, only a small oval of sallow face showing from the strips of linen the priests had used to bind his head.

"Where is Aedan! What have you done with him?"

"Aedan..." said Fulke, now dreamily. "Why, he is in the library studying his maps as always. My foolish daydreaming boy, neglecting his studies. Dreaming over impossible ocean voyages..."

"He's not here, he's gone. No one knows where he is. Tell me, or God help me, I'll pull you from that sickbed and finish you off for good!"

"Let him be, Spaniard!" Paulus snapped, grabbing his arm. "I thought you were gone for good, off to that Portuguese island of yours."

"I did indeed leave, and got as far as Limerick port. But I'm damned if I'll leave Ireland this one last time without my natural son and heir! Where is he?"

Fulke's eyes turned vacant again. "The black witch tried to take him from me, but he is good, pure... in the end he resisted her..."

Jacobo turned to Paulus. "What in the Devil's name is he talking about?"

Paulus turned mournful, then pulled Jacobo from Fulke's beside.

"Aedan has left St. Alban's," he whispered. "We haven't told Lord Fulke yet; we fear the shock would likely kill him."

125

"Where did he go? And what's this about a *witch*?"

Paulus grimaced. "The boy has returned to his home, the island of Inis Ghall."

"His mother's island?"

"Yes!" Paulus' eyes blazed with anger now. "The home of that poor lass you seduced and abandoned and left to die! You don't deserve to be his father, and now you've lost him, too!"

Jacobo ignored the rebuke. "Why would he go *there*? Oh, no." He groaned. "Not to look for that damned *mermaid*! I should never have told him that utterly absurd story! Who'd ever think he'd take it seriously?"

Paulus glowered. "'Tis a serious matter! He was bewitched, indeed, by the black sea-maiden herself. The boy should never have gone there in the first place, he and Lord Fulke. They went to 'investigate.' And our lord comes home deathly ill, and Aedan runs off again. "

"Oh, please. I'm guessing all they found was a brown-haired castaway."

"She is a true witch, with powers from Satan himself Likely she flew here, in raven form, and kidnapped him. He has fallen under her evil spell."

"That is utterly preposterous, man!"

"Something happened to them there. I don't know what, but it is clearly the work of the Devil."

Jacobo approached Fulke once again. "What happened on Inis Ghall? Tell me the truth."

"There is evil there," Fulke murmured, his eyes full of fright. "Until now...I did not know or understand the strength of the dark forces, Lucifer and Satan. I knew only good. I was so arrogant in my modern beliefs. But now I know, Satan has come to curse this part of Eire. He has sent his own mistress, a girl dark as night, whose only goal is conquer good men—"

"Do not talk so, my lord," said, Paulus, deeply distressed.

"It's true, she lives now in that hell which is Connemarra, and Inis Ghall..."

Jacobo turned to Paulus. "I'll sail there and get him, then."

"Go ahead, foreigner. It is no mere Irish isle, but the gate to Hades now. Go ahead and sail there in your mighty ship. You will not find your son, for likely the witch has already taken and drowned him, for her pagan rites. She will kill you and your crew as well."

"You're all crazy," said Jacobo with contempt. "I'm guessing my Aedan has run off with a pretty brunette, and nothing more than that! I will not take him away by force, but I will give him a choice. He can come back here, or come with me to Madeira, to claim his rightful inheritance. Don't worry—I will allow him to come back and say farewell before he goes away...forever! "

Fulke's eyes burned with unholy anger.

"Foreign devil! Spanish Satan! You are only a fornicator, a thief, a vile sinner! Aedan is not yours and never was! He is *my* son—" At this he actually leapt from the bed and flew at Jacobo, flailing at him so violently Paulus was forced to physically restrain him.

"Go!" he shouted back at Jacobo, as he tried to force his superior back onto his sickbed. "Go and claim him if you can! But I'm wagering he won't go with you to Madeira, either! He's beyond anyone's help now!"

But Jacobo chuckled as he left the church ground, walking down to the quays: Those crazy priests! Ranting about dark forces and witches and mermaids! He was pretty sure what had actually happened: Aedan had fallen in love with a dark-haired girl!

He laughed again. He knew Aedan was not meant to be a priest. He was meant to court women, then marry and have children of his own. Be a family man. And with his intelligence, his knowledge of maps, his talent for language, he could become quite the prominent seaman.

But could Jacobo lure the boy away from his siren on the isle of Inis Ghall?

"There's naught to do but try," he told himself. "Why, I'll bring them *both* back to Madeira!"

Before making the brief rescue sail into Galway Bay, which would take less than a half day, Jacobo hurried to the city's market stalls, and began collecting the components of a rich Easter Sunday feast: baskets of exotic candied fruit from abroad, citrus from the Mediterranean, nuts and freshly baked breads and cakes and, of course, the very best Spanish wines: He actually bought back several bottles of his own superb Madeiran wine from his own vineyards, sold to several Galway merchants only weeks before. But the true prize was a succulent, fully-cooked Lough Corrib swan—ordered by an out-of-town chieftain who later changed his mind. Its long neck was said to be the most delicious part. The cooked bird was so enormous Jacobo himself could barely carry it. He had it wrapped in strips of linen and delivered to his carrack in the port, along with the other luxuries. He knew he needed to convince Aedan what delights and pleasures lay ahead of him, as the son of a prosperous Madeiran merchant.

15.

Marra crouched carefully in a corner of the eel-fisher's hut, wary, watchful. In the hearth she tended only the tiniest of fires, a few glowing coals. She did not want smoke from the chimney to betray her presence. Since Anhin and Donnacha had died and were buried, no one from the village dared approached their seaside hut. Marra did not like this hiding place as well as the caves, but she could not go back to that end of the island until the captors' ship had left.

She knew they were looking for her—Urraco and his men. But she would outlast them. Eventually they would weary of the hunt and leave on their ship. She took the pearl from her neck. If they did somehow catch her, she vowed, they would not have it. She picked up a stone on the edge of the hearth, dug a small hole in the earthen floor with her fingers, and placed the pearl there, setting the stone back over it.

Then she curled up by the wan warmth of the coals, and waited for Aedan to return to her. When he came, she would tell him that she had decided to leave the island. She knew now that it was only a short distance from a large mainland. She did not even have to swim through the icy waters to get there, because she had seen that the tides opened a pathway once or twice a day. She would only have to wait until a nighttime parting, then scamper across. There would be more places to hide on the mainland.

She was a little unnerved by the idea. The great-land appeared from Inis Ghall in the daylight as an undulating line of greenery, with a big stone square structure sitting atop a hill. What if wilder, stronger, fiercer peoples lived there? But she was ready to take the chance: it was getting too dangerous, she thought, to remain on the small island any longer. Not only did the captors hate her, but also most of the islanders.

She would not go until the boy Aedan returned. But she had not seen him in two days, not since the night she talked with him at the church; the same night she witnessed the man, Zak-a-row, kill his captain Oo-roko. She had been stunned by this murder, but understood that the men hated their captain, blaming him for all the misery they had been through. She hated him, too, but it was chilling to see him die. She did not like to see people killing other people, no matter what the reason was.

Did Zak-a-row kill Aedan? Please, no, she thought, as she slipped into sleep that night. But

131

when she woke to a cold dawn and dead coals, a sick feeling filled her. He was not coming.

He would have come by now. She creaked the door of the hut open, looking out toward the sea. The Basque ship was still there. Another ship seemed to be approaching far in the distance. More of her captors? It seemed too terrible to be true.

She began immediately to prepare for flight, gathering what she could in one of Donnacha's old eel baskets: Strips of cloth and wool, dried foodstuffs, bits of driftwood collected by Anhin. She paused as she picked up the still sodden remains of a coconut husk. These grew on her island, but not here. How did it get here? She thought there must be hidden trails within the vast ocean, leading from one land mass to another. This coconut must have traveled as she did, west to east, a long journey across the vast sea.

She was still holding the husk when she heard steps, someone approaching the hut. Her heart pounded. Was it Aedan, or a stranger, possibly a pirate? She crouched by the hearth, waiting as the door creaked open. She felt a rush of relief, at the sight of little Koe-lum's bright red hair.

"Marra!" he called to her. She went to meet him, gratefully.

Solemnly, he took her hand, and let her out of doors. He handed her the basket she had just packed, and pointed upshore, toward the caves and west end.

What was he trying to tell her? She stood still, feeling confused. He pushed her, from behind, toward the cliffs.

"Aedan?" she asked, hopefully, turning to him. The boy shook his head sadly, then pointed toward the great mainland. She swallowed hard, instantly understanding. Aedan was gone, off the island. As if to underscore this bitter truth, Colm handed her Donnacha's gray cape. She gripped it, feeling the sting of disappointment in her eyes.

Colm then pulled her up the dunes, and motioned toward the village. She saw, to her horror, fire and black smoke rising from the homes of the islanders. The pirates were now wreaking havoc there, setting fires to the huts in order to flush her out. Soon they would come down to the eel-fisher's hut as well.

Colm took her hand and led her away down the strand toward the cliffs. She did not understand why he was doing this. The sailors had discovered her cliffside hiding place when they dragged Aedan away. They had blocked the entrance with boulders and rocks. Would they not keep returning to see if they could find her there? But Colm trudged ahead in a determined way.

But this time he took her around the back-side of the cliff, a side Marra had not ventured to, as it was covered in thick growth and debris. A plant grew there she knew must be avoided: Just brushing against it would burn the skin like fire, leaving behind welts. Colm bravely forged though the sprouting greenery and pulled it aside.

Behind the growth of stinging nettle and weed was a hole in the rock, another cave. What a clever boy, she thought, astonished he had found something she had not seen before. He ushered her into a small hole, so small she had to stoop double to get in. But once inside, she was astonished to see that the cave ceiling stretched high above her head. The floor of this cave was damp with moisture, but steps had been carved into the side walls, leading to various levels well above the dampness. She realized the entire cliff must be hollow, carved out many centuries before by men looking to hide themselves, or perhaps worship their gods.

Now it was her home again, her refuge. This cave, which did not receive any direct sunlight, was quite dark, but safe. Colm helped her ascend to one of the dry levels, then disappeared; in a little while, he returned with a small iron kettle from Anhin's filled with a few barely glowing embers; and some scraps of food, vegetable peelings and a mutton-bone. He then disappeared again, for the night.

Once again, the fire-haired boy had saved her. If only she could speak with him, but he seemed not to understand the language Aedan called 'Bask.' She was most pleased with his gift of the embers. Now she could have a real, roaring fire, some warmth. She gathered some dry weeds from the mouth of the cave—not the stinging ones—and set her food scraps by the fire to warm up. She spread out Donnacha's cape, to lie down on, and watched the fire leap up and then flicker back down again.

But she soon grew restless within the perpetual night of the cave. She could see the pink and ochre of the evening sky oozing through the fire-hole on the ceiling of the cave, and decided it might be safe to slip out and pick a few fat snails to roast on the fire, perhaps an urchin or two. Wearing only her dingy shift, which now seemed her second skin, she ventured out of the cave and around the front side of the cliff, into an ebb-tide surf, just as the sun was beginning to dip below the horizon. She carefully looked about, but did not see a single other person.

Entranced with the cool beauty of the evening, the bounty of snails and limpets clinging to the seaside rocks, she became oblivious to her surroundings. No one came here, she told herself confidently, only the birds. She took her time and meandered about the boulders and rocks, her mind busily planning her escape from the island. Perhaps she would actually swim across the strait, she thought, since walking across would make her too conspicuous, even at night. Whatever was waiting for her on the mainland could not be worse than what was on this island.

And perhaps Aedan was there, somewhere. The thought of him gave her a pang, and she shook her head roughly, trying to send his image from her brain. He was gone, that was that. She would never be able to find him on that great mainland.

Suddenly, some brute force yanked her backwards, pulling at her hair with such intensity she thought her head might snap. She tried to twist and turn, but she instantly recognized the voice, the language of her attacker —

"Caught you at last, stupid girl!" It was Zak-a-row, the black bearded one, the one who cut Oo-roko's throat. He grabbed at her neck with his other hand. "Give me the pearl. Where is it, you —" Just

135

as his big hand closed about her neck, he suddenly grunted, and let her go, falling into a heap at the surf.

And there stood her golden boy, Aedan, a great stick in one hand, and a stunned look on his face, as if he could not believe what he had just done. But she had no time to embrace him: She saw a small army of the Basque-men running toward them, shouting. She screamed.

"*EEE-Dawwnnnn!*"

"Run!" he cried, in the Basque. "Run, hide yourself again! I'll find you. Go!" He pushed her away just as the men were almost on them. He let them swarm over him, knocking him into the surf with Zak-a-row.

Having no where else to go, she dashed and dove headlong into the waves and sea, swimming out into the frigid water as far as she could.

But the men took no notice: Zachario was just coming to, and his men began tying Aedan up once again.

"This time we keep you prisoner," Zachario muttered. "We'll see what the girl likes better. Her damned pearl, or you."

16.

The Basques kept Aedan tied up with twine in Father Comgall's room alongside the church, while the priest and his family watched helplessly. Through the night, Zachario interrogated him relentlessly in Spanish, though Aedan could not tell him what he wanted to know.

"Talk, spoiled-brat priests' boy! Where does your sweetheart hide out, other than the caves?"

"I don't know!"

"What are you planning to do with her?"

"I have no plans for her!"

"What did she do with the pearl? Do you have it?"

"No! What do you want from me? I don't know where it is!"

"What do we want from you?" Zachario unsheathed his pocket blade. "You are our worm, our fishing lure. We are fishermen, so we are using you as bait, to attract the mermaid." He pointed the blade at Aedan. "We will do whatever it takes, kill you if necessary. Because it seems the dark girl has become quite attached to you."

Aedan stared at the knife blade. The hilt was stained with a crusty darkness. He stared at the blade, then up at Zachario.

She did not kill Urroco Vizkiero. You did, he thought.

"You know nothing about her, do you," Zachario continued. "She could be a wanton murderer. A cannibal, for all you know. She is from a strange island, on the other side of the world. Her people go about naked, and swim like fish. They have no Church there, no government, no morals or code. She is a wild creature, untamed and unlearned, dangerous. Is that what you want in a girlfriend?"

Aedan looked him in the eyes. "I am not afraid of her. Or of you."

"We'll see." He left Aedan to sleep, still fettered in twine. But in the morning, Aedan was roughly awakened.

"Take the boy outside," Zachario barked to his countrymen. "Tie him to the stake so conveniently set up there."

Comgall raced over as they tied Aedan, shirtless, to the stake that had been erected in front of the church.

"What are they doing? Surely they're not going to burn you!"

"Tell the bumpkin priest," said Zachario, drily, to Aedan, "that I am merely trying to attract the attention of a certain maiden. This was the week our Lord was crucified. You, too, shall remain here for three hours. If your lover-girl does not turn up, we will light the kindling beneath you. That should get her attention."

Comgall approached Aedan. "Why didn't you stay in Galway?! You should never have returned!" But his face was full of sorrow, not reproach.

"I could not let her die, uncle, nor any more of you. I had to return, that's all there is to it."

"We must find that girl and bring her here," said the priest. "To save your life."

"No!" Aedan cried. "Let her be. No more harm can come to her. She has suffered enough."

"You would *die*, to save this mere girl's life?"

"I don't want to die, uncle. But if nothing else, I have learned my lessons well at St. Alban's. To lay down one's life for another is the greatest gift. I will do it, if it means she will be safe."

"You are monstrously brave, my boy. A true Irishman at heart. Or, maybe a fool." Comgall dashed back into his own quarters, awakening his young son:

"Colm! Where is the dark girl?"

Colm did not answer, but looked away.

"I won't punish you. But you must go find her, bring her here, or your cousin Aedan will die. "

"Then *she* will die, too," Colm cried.

"She is nothing to you, but this boy is your family. Your blood. You must save him."

Cole gazed dolefully at his father for a long moment, then ran off. He ran across the sheep meadow toward the western shore, bounding along the rock-strewn coast toward the pagan cliff. He stopped briefly at Anhin's hut. The thatched roof had been burnt off completely, leaving the interior within the stone walls gaping up into the sky.

He continued to run, faster now. Then he suddenly stopped short again.

The pirate's carrack, with its tattered sails, still sat offshore. But now there was another ship coming in just behind it. He stared. Unlike the pirate's vessel, this new ship was in fine shape, with brand-new painted sails in red and blue and yellow. The ship was coming directly toward the island.

Were the pirates bringing in reinforcements?

He ran down to the cliffs, now shouting her name: "Marra! Marra!"

He peered into the hidden cave, but saw no one there.

"Marra!" He circled round to the front of the cliff-face.

"Koe-lum? Koe-lum." He heard her voice, a low melody amid the raucous cackling of the seabirds. He turned and saw her crouched by one of the big boulders at the sea's edge, partly disguised by Anhin's big brown cloak. He beckoned to her, but she would not move. He ran down to the surf and grabbed her hand. And at first, perhaps sensing his intention, she would not budge, shaking her head.

"Aedan!" he cried. "Aedan needs you. Please, Marra. Come now."

At this she immediately rose and slowly followed him up the beach and over the dunes, through the sheep meadow and into the small village in the heart of Inis Ghall.

Meanwhile, Zachario and his band were growing restless. Father Comgall's remaining parishioners, those who had survived the island epidemic of fever, were gathering now around the stake, observing Aedan's plight with curiosity and concern. Some shouted at him, trying to talk to him, and Zachario knocked them back with impatience.

"Enough of this nonsense," he snapped. "I'm not waiting any longer, I'm lighting this fire now. Let's burn the boy-witch and see how much his girl loves him after all. Who will donate a burning coal from their hearth?"

The crowd, not understanding his language, simply stared at him.

"You'll get no help from them," Aedan shouted. "You've burned their homes, brought them fever." He was trying very hard now to be brave, but inside he was almost sick with terror. It looked as if he may well die. What would it be like to be consumed by fire? A cold trickle of sweat ran down his bare back.

And what would the Lord Almighty say to him on the Judgment seat? Would He rebuke Aedan, for forsaking his Lord Fulke, renouncing his studies? Would he be condemned to everlasting burning, forever?

"Never mind," Zachario muttered. "I'll do this myself." He took out a flint-stone and knocked it against a rock, near a patch of grass by the stake. A spark leapt into the dried hay by the foot of the stake and turned instantly into hungry flame. The crowd gasped and Aedan squeezed his eyes shut, and began murmuring the prayer of contrition—

Oh my Lord, I am heartily sorry, for having offended Thee —

Suddenly Marra herself flew into their midst, Anhin's dun cloak flapping behind her, her long strands of black hair wild in the wind. A collective gasp rose up from the crowd: This was the first time the 'dark witch' had been seen out in the open in daylight, and the sight of her was startling to many, her brown skin, her coal-dark hair, her broad face and foreign cheekbones.

Father Comgall moved through the crowd to get to her before others did. He took her by the shoulders and she gasped for breath, her chest heaving from the effort of running across the island. Tears sparkled in her eyes and her bronzed cheeks were stained pink with flush. *She's just a lass, for Lord's sake,* thought Comgall, overcome with pity for her. Perhaps a girl in her teens, fresh and pretty in her own way.

"Aedan!" she cried. She raced toward the fire, throwing her cloak over the flame. It seemed an odd thing to do, but it quelled the fire.

Aedan opened his eyes. "Marra?" he murmured, weakly.

But someone, one of the islanders, grabbed at her hair, pulling her back roughly. "The sea witch! This is the witch that's caused our misery! Burn her!"

Both islanders and pirates were swarming about her now. "The pearl," Zachario shouted. "Where is the damned pearl?"

Meanwhile, the hay had somehow re-ignited at the edge of the cloak, and Aedan, still tied to the stake, watched the growing flames with horror. He tried to kick at the kindling with his feet, trying to drive the fire away, as the crowd continued to scuffle over Marra, who was shrieking now.

And suddenly an explosion shook the island, a great thunderclap of a boom. Screaming, everyone, pirates and islanders alike, fell to the ground. Only Marra remained standing; she ran to Aedan and again extinguished the flame by moving her cloak. A milky fog reeking of sulfurous smoke hovered the entire scene.

Only a few leagues away stood a legion of brilliantly dressed foreigners, clustered about a strange object that continued to spew blue-gray smoke: A cylinder of iron, set on a scaffolding of varnished wooden boards. The smell of brimstone and sulfur remained in the air.

Aedan cried out, with joy.

"Father! It is my own father, Jacobo de Adamo, who has come to save us!"

17.

On the day after the Spanish wine merchant de Adamo's visit to St. Alban's, Lord Fulke rose from his sick bed, much to the apprehension and concern of the other priests and brothers. It was clear to them he was not close to recovery at all, and it was painful to see their once vital and graceful vicar struggling to his feet and lurching about the halls. He was dreadfully thin and pale as any tomb dweller. But he seemed determined to be out of his sickbed, and not all of his memory had left him.

The city and abbey resounded with the sound of bells: It was the great feast of Easter, the celebration of the Lord Jesus' resurrection. But Fulke walked his halls like a mourner.

"How many days now?" he demanded of Brother Paulus, the only person he seemed to recognize.

"What do you mean, lord?"

"How many days has our child Aedan been gone?"

"Ah." Paulus gave him a look of sadness. "Only a few. But too many, for us to bear."

"Why have you not gone out to find him?"

Paulus paused. "He is not lost, m'lord. He chose to leave us."

"That is not possible, not possible..." Fulke muttered fretfully, wheezing and coughing as he did so. "He is only lost, our little lamb. We must go and find him."

"No, m'lord," said Paulus, gently. "You are not well enough to leave the abbey. You should go and rest."

"How can I rest when my son is lost? How can I sleep, or eat, when my son has been taken from me!"

"Please, Lord Fulke—"

Fulke suddenly swung as if to strike him. Paulus moved to gently restrain his hand, but was profoundly shocked. He had never known his superior to show any kind of physical violence to anyone.

"I say, we will go! Now!"

"My lord, there is no point is such a journey!" Paulus struggled to restrain him. "Don't you remember, his father was just here yesterday to look for him. Likely he has found him and—"

"He is in peril!" Fulke cried, in a high-pitched shriek. "He is in danger, mortal danger, my son Aedan! We must go!"

"Have you forgotten your duties here, my lord? It is Easter Sunday! You must recover, you have a church and school to run, many other things to do—"

"None of that matters. Nothing matters anymore...now that Aedan is gone."

"I'll go myself, lord, and I'll bring him back."

"No. I shall go!" Fulke staggered off toward the front gates. "I will go, if I have to crawl to that cursed island on my stomach!"

Paulus quickly consulted with the other priests, who all agreed: Lord Fulke had gone mad. What could be done? He was their superior, so they could not physically restrain him, or imprison him in his own church.

"He will likely die," said one of the more pragmatic priests. "Will it matter to the Almighty if he dies in his bed, or on the road to Inis Ghall?"

"True enough," said Paulus. "There is nothing to do but take him. I am quite sure as soon as the trip grows hard, he will give it up. In any case, perhaps if the boy sees what his lord has endured for his sake, mayhaps he will return with us to Galway."

"Or, it could push our sire over the edge for good," another muttered. "What do you think has become of young Aedan?"

Paulus sighed. "He is a still a boy, foolish and eager. We coddled him, protected him too much. I fear he is on his way to Madeira now with the Spaniard, ready to taste the fruits of the world. I fear he has forgotten us all already. "

In the morning, Paulus procured a small donkey from a merchant to carry Fulke into the Irish hinterlands. The vicar of St. Alban's was a frightening sight, even bundled into his embroidered velvet cloak of scarlet, only his sallow skull-like visage peeking out from the folds of fabric. He was hunched precariously atilt on the beast, riding through the narrow alleys of Galway in a strange parody of his Lord and Savior's Palm

Sunday ride through Jerusalem. But none of the Galwegians shouted *Hosanna* at Fulke; all looked away, in dismay.

As Paulus predicted, the journey was arduous enough. They were soaked by a brief and violent rain, and many times the beast carrying Lord Fulke would stop short and refuse to go on. Sometimes it seemed Fulke was about to totter and fall onto the road, and Paulus grew nearly faint with the exertion of it all, for he was not a young man himself.

But some strange, brimming energy within Fulke kept him going, kept him on the donkey, his eyes focused tightly on the western horizon. When they came to the crossing point, just below the O hEynne's rectangular fortress, it seemed the ocean had obligingly parted just for them, a narrow sandy path dotted with winkles and blue mussels, snaking toward the small isle. Sunset stained the western sky.

"Stop," said Fulke, rather calmly, somewhat to Paulus' surprise. It seemed the trip, difficult as it was, had a therapeutic effect on Fulke, who seemed to be regaining some of his former self.

"Sir, we are here," said Paulus. "We need only to cross the strait and be on Inis Ghall."

"No. We are not going to Inis Ghall tonight. Take me up to the fortress of the O hEynne. We will rest under the protection of the chieftain, Murtogh. I need to speak with him again. I have much to tell him, much to warn him about."

18.

All it took to drive the Basque pirates from Inis Ghall was the sight of Jacobo de Adamo's hand-cannon, the latest innovation in war technology borrowed from the Turks and Arabs. And, a few careful words in Basque, from Jacobo himself.

"I merely suggested that the local Irish chieftains were unlikely to be pleased with their presence here. And that thousands of bloodthirsty tribes were just waiting across the strait to chop off their heads and wear them on their belts! And if that wasn't enough to scare them away, I might be forced to blow them to bits with my new weapon!" Jacobo explained jovially. He chuckled. "I doubt they'll be able to get much further in that rotting, leaky hulk of theirs. They'll be lucky if they make it to Brittany. Now." He turned to his son. "Where is this famous mermaid, this dark maiden?"

Aedan looked about, but Marra was gone.

"She...she must have gone back into hiding. I think your hand-cannon frightened her."

"Well, she can't have gone far. It's a small island. Come, it's Easter, let's celebrate the holiday. And, my reunion with my only dear son."

Laid out on Father Comgall's humble oak table was the most extraordinary meal the priest and his family had ever seen. Fine-grained white bread, fresh salad vegetables, sweetmeats, oranges and citron from Araby, dried dates coated in sugar, almonds, and the centerpiece, a huge fully-cooked Lake Corrib swan, the meat of Irish kings and noblemen. All to be washed down with the heavenly sweet wine of Spain and Madeira. Comgall and his children were agog at the feast, the likes of which they had never seen before.

"And to think we were planning on a simple stew of cockles and mussels," said Comgall to Aedan, between bites of succulent swan. "No lambs were tithed to us this Easter, and even our root cellar is completely empty! This is a miracle indeed!"

Aedan had been astonished and delighted at the sudden reappearance of his father, but as he sat at the Easter dinner with the others, found himself still trying to digest the crushing news his father had just given him a few moments earlier.

"Your Lord Fulke is quite ill, dying of the fever he contracted here," Jaocbo had told his son. "I fear he may already have passed on, as we speak."

Aedan had literally sunk to the ground, in remorse. Fulke, his adopted father, dead, gone from this world? All because they had come to Inis Ghall, and partly at Aedan's own prompting—

"It's not your fault about the vicar," Jacobo said now at the table, guessing his son's thoughts. "Why did he succumb to the fever while you did not? It must be the will of God."

149

"I suppose," Aedan murmured. "But if anyone should have died of that fever, it should have been me."

"Indeed," said Comgall, between bites of his dinner. The conversation was being conducted in Irish, for his benefit. "After your nights with the dark girl, I fully expected you would."

"Nights with the dark girl!" Jacobo raised his eyebrows. "What's this!"

"I don't want to speak of her now." Aedan turned his head away. He felt a mixture of shame, sorrow for Lord Fulke — a sense of having betrayed the holy man — and yet, a longing to see Marra again. The pirates were gone now, but she was still in danger from the island folk, eager to make her pay for the inconvenience of having to deal with the Basque men.

He calmed himself with the thought that she was safe somewhere. She was an intelligent, resourceful girl, and she'd be safe at the pagan end of the island, where no islander would dare go. It was only a matter of time before he was reunited with her again.

"The pirates told me a curious thing," Jacobo continued. "They were looking not so much for the girl, but for a pearl."

Aedan nodded, but Colm suddenly spoke up. "She wore it around her neck." He licked the sticky remains of date-sugar off his fingers, then reached into the neckline of his own tunic. "Here it is!"

"How did you get that!" Aedan exclaimed.

Colm handed it to him. "Marra hid it under a stone in the hearth in Anhin's hut. After the pirates burnt the roof off, I went in and looked for it. You can give it back to her when you see her."

"Let me see that, son." Jacobo took the pearl in his fingers. "Extraordinary! It's huge!" He grinned at his son. "What about the girl? Is she just as extraordinary?"

Aedan flushed, took the pearl back from his father, but did not answer. Jacobo began talking to him in a low voice, in Basque.

"A father should tell his son these things. You are still young yet, although old enough to marry if you choose. But you should not marry until you are past twenty. Until then, you may frolic with the girls, but choose wisely. If you get a girl with child, you will have to marry her. And many girls are not worth marrying. You must find a suitable girl, of noble birth and good breeding."

Aedan merely stared at his father, unable to answer him.

"You left the abbey, now you must start thinking like a man of the world. Be a man, for heaven's sake!"

"I don't know what that means," Aedan replied. "If being a man means making wise choices, being responsible...I am not one yet. " He shook his head. "How much my life has changed, since I came to this island! I can't go back to my former life, but I don't know what is coming next for me. I no longer know what true path my life is to take."

Jacobo put his hand on Aedan's shoulder. "I, for one, cannot help but see the hand of Fortune, in all of this."

"How so?"

"I cannot tell you why I came back to Galway. When you did not show up that morning, I was angry and told my crew to set sail immediately. We got as far as Limerick, when I reconsidered. I had not been fair to you, giving you only a night to decide. It wasn't enough time. But I realize now that the fates were pushing me back in this direction, so I could again offer you a new life. And, a future."

Aedan stared at him.

"Son, you cannot refuse me this second time. And we must go at once, since the rest of my fleet is docked in Limerick port, waiting for my return. I won't force you. But I do have a good life to offer you. Be honest. Do you wish to spend the rest of your life here, on this isle of Ghall?"

"I...don't know."

"The answer is simple. You must come with me."

"But what about Marra?"

"Go and find her," said Jacobo, in a casual way. "Find her, and we will bring her with us. Her, and her extraordinary pearl."

Aedan left Comgall's dwelling in late afternoon, as the others napped off their heavy dinner. He had taken some of the exotic fruits and swan-meat for Marra to feast on as well. It was suddenly clear to him what he must do.

I must *marry* her, he thought: It was the only way she could be completely safe. But first I will have to convert her, he thought, make her a Christian. I will have to teach her the ways of Europe, how to wear proper women's clothes. I will teach her English and Irish, and Spanish and Portuguese, too, especially if they were going to live on his father's sunny isle of Madeira. He smiled. She would like that island much better than Ghall—it would be warm always, green and fruitful, with a benign sea to swim in. They would live in a real house, not a cave by the sea.

And she will be my companion, for the rest of my days. That thought gave Aedan intense joy, the thought of Marra and her gentle smile with him, forever. And maybe one day, they would sail west, and find the island of her birth...

The afternoon sun, brilliant gold-amber, pierced through a cloud of lavender gray; and the magical light over the ocean seemed to him an omen, a sign from Heaven. Yes, this is what the Almighty Lord wanted for him: It had not been the priesthood after all. The priests of St. Alban's had merely been the gentle caretakers of his youth, preparing him for a great life they could not possibly imagine: That of a great seafarer, explorer. And husband, father.

He ran down to the surf, scanning the waves and rocks and bobbing seabirds. Mercifully the pirate ship was long gone, only Jacobo's cheerful carrack sitting just offshore, its colorful sails fluttering in the breeze.

"Marra!" he shouted, but the wind carried off his words. He had to find her, to start their new life! "Marra!" he called again, but he was answered only by shrieking birds.

He ran to the cliffs, his heart pounding. The arch at the top was still partly blocked by stones and boulders set there by the Basques. He scrambled up the side of the cliff, then began pulling at the stones, throwing them over the cliff, onto the beach below. "Marra, Marra!" he cried. "I'm here! Where are you?" He scrambled through the arched doorway, stumbling, then falling into the dark emptiness beyond.

The cave was empty, the once fiery hearth he had slept beside Marra with, cold. He looked back out the door, out at the setting sun, the stain of colors on the waves. And then he saw her.

She stood at the base of the cliff, looking up at him, her face shining, smiling, golden with the light of the dying day. In her linen shift she was amber and pink, glowing like her pearl, her hair black and sleek on her shoulders.

"Marra," he whispered. Immediately, she began to climb up toward him, expertly navigating the narrow ledges and footholds. Withing moments, she was standing before him, somewhat damp from the surf, her dark eyes intensely focused on his.

Feeling suddenly shy, strange, he placed his hands on her arms, which were cold to the touch, bumpy with goose-flesh. He began rubbing her arms, then embraced her against himself, whispering in Basque: *Let me warm you.*

She let him embrace her awhile but then stepped back herself, a little fearfully, as if she were afraid of what he might do next.

"I won't hurt you, Marra," he said softly, taking her hand. "I only want to be with you. I want you to be my wife."

"Wife?" She frowned at this unfamiliar word.

"Marriage? Husband? Family?"

She continued to frown.

"Be with me. Always."

She smiled. "I be with you, Aedan."

She was delighted with the food he brought: She devoured the oranges and dates immediately, laughing.

"Good," she said. "Good to eat."

"Do you have fruits like these on your island?"

"No. But these are good. They are of Ire-land?" She knew now, the name of the country where she had landed.

"Oh no! Oranges cannot grow in Eire! They are from Araby, to the south of here. I guess you are not Arabian, or Asian. Or African. Where are you from, Marra?"

"I tell you. Hot land, to the west. With many, many plants, Flowers and fruit, birds and insect. Iguana. The pearl clam and big pink snail we use for horn." She rose and moved to the entrance of the cave, pointing out into the semi-darkness.

He studied the direction she pointed in. Not quite west, more toward the south. South and west, from Eire. He felt a light dawning in his brain, as the sun slipped below the horizon. His father's island of Madeira lay in that direction. Beyond that isle, Jacobo told him the air grew hotter still. In Africa, he said, the dark-skinned natives went about without clothes, because it was so hot. But he did not think Marra was from Africa, thinking she did not resemble the pictures he'd seen of those peoples in his books.

155

There must be, he thought, a land directly due west of Morroque and the Sahara, something that corresponded with Africa in climate. How far was it? How many days? Perhaps it would not be a difficult trip to make out of Madeira's port, often a stopping-over point for ships bound for Africa's coast.

And what was that land? It must be part of the Indies, he thought with conviction. It was likely part of the great empire of Cathay or perhaps Cipangu,' described many years before by the explorer Marco Polo.

He understood now: Marra was not from one of Brendan's Blessed Isles or any western island, but possibly from the farthest *East*, the spice islands of India and the Asian subcontinent! That would also explain her pearl, since the most majestic pearls were said to come from that area. She was living proof that beyond the great Western Sea, the earth did not drop off into a black void.

This knowledge, he knew, was *huge*. It had enormous implications for European commerce and travel. It could have huge consequences for his father's own business—if Jacobo sent a fleet due west and south, to trade for these fabulous pearls, and perhaps other luxuries of the tropics, he could make an incredible fortune. He would have untold power, and influence, in the courts of Europe.

His reveries in the library of St. Alban's had not been feeble schoolboy dreams.

"My father says there are no lands to the far west," he told Marra. "He is wrong!" He took her hand. "Tell me more, about your land. About you."

She then told him her tale, as best as she could in her imperfect Euskera, using gestures, facial expressions and carefully chosen words to describe her story. As he guessed, it was far different than Urraco's rather graphic and fanciful version. She told him of how she had been a pearl-fisher with her father, of her gentle little lagoon and her gentle people, but also of the fierce tribes who lived south, the tribes who killed her mother and brothers. She told him of her father, who she had loved so much, and how he taught her many things. How she and her father had been fishing together far out in the ocean beyond their lagoon, too far, and how Urraco's ship had come from nowhere, dragging them up out of their canoe. How Urraco killed her father, so quickly. And then the terrible voyage, and the drifting of the ship into ice. The fever that raged aboard the ship. But also, how she learned Basque, by carefully listening to the sailors.

"...and I see the Ireland, the land, I go to escape. I climb up, I shut eyes, I jump in water. Ask sea god, to be good with me."

"Here, we have only one God."

"More is better," she replied. "Gods everywhere. In sea, land. Caves." She squinted at Aedan, in a curious way. "You story now. You, not from...here."

"No. I mean, yes. I was born here. My mother is of this island, these people. My father...he is of another land."

"Place of my captors."

"Yes."

"Your mother and father....they....marriage?" She put her hands together.

"No. They—" He stopped short, remembering what Jacobo had told him.

Some girls are not worth marrying.

"No," he continued, slowly. "My mother was his *whore*." In Basque, the word was *puta*.

Mara hung her head. "I know that word," she said. "They call me that, on ship."

"Did they...did they touch you, Marra, hurt you in bad way—"

"With their man parts? They try to grab at me, touch me...my father save me, fight them for me. But they kill him. I hide away from them. Protect myself. Later, they all too sick, too busy..."

Aedan shuddered, realizing she was describing how she somehow managed to avoid being brutally raped on board the ship. Even though the Basque and Spanish men onboard that ship were Christians, he knew they would not hesitate to try and force themselves on a defenseless young woman, even if it was one of the worst kinds of sin. They'd killed their own captain!

"Those cretins! You are no *puta*, Marra. You are fine, and good. And beautiful!"

She smiled. "You beautiful too."

He laughed. "But I am too tall, too thin...and I feel so pale, next to you!"

"You mother," she prompted. "She is here?"

"No, she is dead."

"Father kill her?"

"No! She died when I was born. My birth...made her die. Do you understand?"

She nodded, gravely.

"She may not have died, had my father married her. He could have taken her back to the city, where she could have gotten good care."

"Your father is bad."

"No. He is…not bad. But he did not raise me. I had another father. A man who took care of me, named Fulke. He was a very, very good man. I loved him, very much." He bit his lip. How could he explain, in the simplest Basque, the complexities of his upbringing, life at St. Alban's, his former vocation? "This man Fulke, he was a priest. Do you know what that is?"

"Man who talk to gods. One on ship, but he die."

"This man Fulke was a priest. And he wanted me to be a priest, too."

Her eyes lit up. "You will talk with your gods? Make sacrifice?"

"No. In our world, priests do not marry women, or have children. Except for my uncle Comgall, the priest of this island. He is a good man, but not a very good priest. He has two children."

"Koe-lum?"

"Yes, Colm is his son. Colm is my cousin, too, my family."

"That Koe-lum, he good boy. I like."

"That reminds me, where is your pearl?"

Stricken, she placed a hand to her chest, her eyes widening. But she dissolved into relieved laughter as Aedan dangled it before her. She snatched it eagerly.

"Colm found it."

She immediately tied it back around her neck. "Is…my home, my island."

He understood. It was all she had left of that faraway isle.

"I will take you there one day, Marra. Back to your home faraway."

"No," she said, softly. "No go."

"You don't want to go back there?"

"No, I cannot. I never go ship again. Ship is evil, bad."

"Not all ships are bad. My father's ship—that one outside, just offshore—It's a good ship, with good men."

"No," Marra insisted. "I not go. I stay here now, in Ireland."

"You cannot stay here on Inis Ghall. The islanders wish you harm."

"I not go ship. We walk."

"Let's not talk of this right now. I will discuss this with you in the morning." He rose to go, but she reached out to him.

"Aedan. Not go."

"I must…I cannot stay with you all night."

"I hate dark. Cold…"

She beckoned to him, to come and lie beside her, under the cloaks. There was his nice warm green cloak, which he had left here before. He lingered a moment by the mouth of the cave, then went back to join her, in the flickering light of the dying fire in the small hearth. Under the cloaks, they leaned into each other, and he felt her heartbeat against his. She gazed into his eyes, trusting, loving.

He placed his lips against her cheek, as she had done with him at the church. Her skin was astonishing, so soft and warm beneath his mouth. "Oh, Marra," he murmured. "Marra, *mo rún*," he whispered, in Irish. It was an old Gaelic word, *rún*, a soft croon of a word, *roo-ooon*, a word he had never spoken before, nor had reason to use. It meant 'mystery' or 'secret', but also, sweetheart, *my love*.

19.

The castle fortress of the O hEynne clan sat atop a cliff overlooking the far western edge of Galway Bay, a great spare stone rectangle surrounded by ancient yews. The castle's inhabitants, the chieftain Murtogh O hEynne and his huge extended family, were largely oblivious to the current chaos on their island territory of Ghall. The chieftain was much more concerned with matters of home repair and neighborly relations. Just two hundred years old, the stone tower was already falling into decay, its limestone blocks slipping askew after seeing two centuries of near-constant clan warfare. The fortress lay in a difficult spot, squarely within territory claimed by the both the O Flaithertaigh and the O Mallaigh tribes, neither of whom thought much of the O hEynnes, who were steadily losing their influence in that part of Connemarra.

This local band of O hEynne managed to soldier on despite a perplexing and potentially serious genealogical problem: A lack of sons. Murtogh had already sired ten surviving daughters, but not a single male. That meant ten dowries, and ten less warriors for the battles he still needed to fight occasionally. His wife was well past forty years now, and unlikely to produce any more children, thus indicating the end of the O hEynne name in that part of Connemarra. Worse yet, his daughters were not gentle sedate obedient creatures, content to sit and learning spinning and embroidery from the nuns, but wild creatures much taken with the hounds and the horses they loved to race across the landscape of Connemarra. And who was Murtogh supposed to marry them all off to? Certainly not to an O Mallaigh or an O Flaithertaigh!

Murtogh O hEynne was a man with many worries indeed. He was not pleased, therefore, to hear that a pair of ecclesiastical visitors from Galway city had turned up on his doorstep the day after Easter. He had his own cleric, his own chapel for the celebration of Easter Week. He was not up to entertaining strangers, no matter how holy they might be.

But the clerics, a priest and professed brother from tiny St. Alban's in the city, insisted on meeting with him. He had just entertained a priest from that church, a strange fellow named Fulke, who'd been fulminating about some student of his lost on Inis Ghall. Murtogh had concluded that the boy merely saw the opportunity to run away from his strict old teacher and he sent the cleric on his way. So who were these two idiots, he groused, showing up during such an important week in the Church year? Why weren't they home, tending to their own business?

Murtogh decided to teach them a lesson by not greeting them immediately. He told his servants to settle them into the guests' hut some distance from the castle proper, with instructions to feed them regularly and tell them that he would greet them when he had the first opportunity to do so.

This did not come for two days; in fact, Murtogh had completely forgotten about the existence of the visitors until reminded by one of his servants. With an exasperated sigh, he heaved himself out in the direction of the hut, accompanied by his ever-loyal gang of barking hounds.

He had at least taken care to ensure that the visitors received decent food and drink, some mutton and dark bread, nothing fancy, and good dark ale from his stores. Nevertheless, they greeted him with glum, affronted faces. One—the one wearing the red embroidered cape of a rich priest—resembled more a skeleton than a man, while the other was reassuringly Irish-looking, with a bald pate and the distinct look of someone who had been coerced into doing something unpleasant.

They in turn confronted a man of considerable stature and girth, with unfashionably short-clipped hair and a bushy brown-gray beard—all *civilized*, Norman, men were shaving their chins—but his corpulent, big-bellied frame had been squeezed into the latest in Galway male fashion (insisted upon by his wife), a tight yellow-striped jacket and green-satin breeches. The ancient and traditional Irish shirt-garment, the white-linen *leine*, with its voluminous sleeves, poked out at odd places. Murtogh brushed some crumbs of bread and cheese from his beard, and frowned at the visitors.

"I meant no true offense at keeping you waiting. But you came at an awkward time, understand? What did you want?"

"You do not recognize me, Murtogh O hEynne?" said the skeleton. "It is I, Lord Fulke, who only recently spent several nights under your roof."

Murtogh gasped. The man's appearance had changed so—in just a matter of days!—he could not believe his eyes. It scared him.

"What happened to you, man?"

Fulke ignored the inquiry. "We are back to warn you of possible disaster, here on your own lands."

For a frightening moment, Murtogh wondered if the clergyman had transformed into the fabled Angel of Death, coming for his own soul. He glanced at the brother, who merely sat with his chin on his hand.

"What's this about?" he snapped, ignoring the convention that one should be polite to visiting priests and clergy. But he was not in a good mood. "Must we speak in English?" he demanded, hating that damned effeminate language used in Galway city.

"I assure you this is no frivolous mission." The skeleton Fulke seemed lordly and gentlemanly enough, but his red-rimmed pale eyes burned with the intensity of a madman.

"You are about to be invaded and overcome, your lands and castle taken from you."

"What?! That's nonsense. Did the O Flaithertaigh send you here?"

"No. It is no native Irish tribe that threatens you, but a band of foreigners. Indeed, they have already claimed your island of Inis Ghall and have set up operations there. Likely, your mainland stronghold is next."

"Ghall! That craphole!" As far as Murtogh was concerned, the island was nothing, nothing but mud and bog and a giant rock off the coast, full of idiot inbred fishermen. He'd heard dim rumors of a sickness there, but it mattered not to him. Inis Ghall was worthless real estate, good only for oysters and cockles and the fat eels that slithered in its strait. "What sort of foreigners?"

"Spaniards," said Fulke, calmly, and this gave Murtogh considerable pause. The Spanish were a world power, as important as France or England. He knew that a few of them came up to Galway to trade their wines and had seen them at the port there, but had given them little thought.

"I tell you, they are planning to launch some sort of attack. First on you and your holdings. Then on to the other clans. Soon Ireland will be New Spain and we'll be forced to speak their singsong language and pay tithes to the Spanish King. Your daughters will become concubines in the harems of the Moors."

Murtogh stared at him, incredulous. "Priest, I have to tell you...it sounds preposterous."

"The owner of the ship," Fulke continued, "is a wealthy and powerful Castilian nobleman named Jacobo de Adamo. He has recently seized part of the new island of Madeira in the Atlantic, and seeking to set up an empire for himself."

"And you know this...how?"

"He has a son in Ireland, sired with an Inis Ghall girl, and that is why he chose that island, to set up a kingdom there for his boy."

"Oh, the boy again. Let me guess, your wayward student. Didn't turn up, eh? Does it occur to you that he just might not want to be a priest like you?"

Fulke lunged at Murtogh, grabbing the tail of his *leine*, his red eyes wild. "Wake up, man! De Adamo has his own forces, weapons, untold wealth! How long do you think it will take him to move to the mainland and claim your lands too?"

Murtogh frowned. The clergyman's tale, if true, could be quite troubling. A foreign ship off Inis Ghall. He didn't like that, he didn't like it one bit.

"But that is not the only trouble you face," Fulke intoned.

"There's *more*?"

The priest Fulke was now shaking, quivering. He grabbed onto a bench and lowered himself down with great effort.

"I've been ill, you can see. An illness I contracted on Inis Ghall."

"I heard something about a fever."

"It is no mere fever, but a *plague* that kills most of its victims. It nearly killed me, but I had too much spiritual strength for it, the warriors of God on my side."

"There's *plague* on Inis Ghall?!" Murtogh was old enough to remember the last plague epidemic in Galway city, which killed hundreds of people, dead bodies left in the alleys. He felt a deep chill.

"Yes. We know plague comes and goes, but this particular plague has a cause, an agent of destruction. A female, who brought this evil illness to your unsuspecting island to kill off all its inhabitants and all the rest of us as well."

"A Spanish woman?"

"No, no! This woman is not of this world, but of the world below us. She is a minion of Satan himself."

"I think you might possibly be insane, man."

Fulke glowered at him. "I assure you I am not, but an educated priest of God. You, your family and entire clan are in mortal danger. Not only from the temporal forces of the Spanish, but from the dark forces of Lucifer himself, who is trying to use your small island to wreak havoc on Ireland and the rest of the world!"

Murtogh now turned to the taller man named Paulus. "Tell me, you. Tell me in Irish. Is this true?"

Paulus looked uncomfortable. "If Lord Fulke says so," he replied, obediently, but his eyes told Murtogh a different story. They seemed to be signaling to him: *The priest is stark raving mad but I have to go along with him, because he's my boss.* "I might point out, there *is* a ship anchored off Inis Ghall. We saw it as we were coming here, but you cannot because it is behind the western cliffs, so you cannot see it from your tower. It is not an English ship, and has yellow, red and blue sails. It is quite impressive."

"Hmmm." Murtogh looked at him, then at the feverish skeleton man, trying to size up the situation. He was not much educated himself, he could not read nor write more than his own initials, but he prided himself on a kind of primitive intuition he believed he had inherited from his pagan warrior ancestors. He might not be as bold or crazily impetuous as other Irish chieftains before him, and certainly not as bloodthirsty: He liked to think of himself as 'modern.' He tried to make careful decisions, ensuring the welfare of his clan. But once convinced action was needed, it would be all-out bloody war. He had a large band of loyal warriors at hand, mostly cousins and second-cousins and distant family members. They no longer hacked off the heads of their enemies, as his forefathers had, pickling them in vats of cedar-oil. But Murtogh himself had no qualms about killing or hurting anybody he thought was a threat to his clan or property.

Yet this talk of Satin, witches…Here he felt in deep water, over his head. He retained some of his family's old superstitions, and did not doubt the existence of such things. But how were such things dealt with these days? Surely one needed more than hatchets and axes.

"There's a Spanish ship off Inis Ghall," he said carefully, to himself. "There's plague and possibly a witch loose, wreaking havoc. " Then, to Fulke, in English: "Mayhaps, the witch will kill off the Spaniards! Problem solved, eh?"

"This is a far darker, more threatening situation than you can possibly understand," Fulke murmured, in a voice that chilled Murtogh to the core. "We may indeed be witness to the very end of our world."

"What do you suggest *I* do, priest?"

Fulke stared at him for a long, long moment, then shut his eyes, as if in agony. "Give me a moment," he muttered. "My bones, my flesh are giving out...I will not inhabit this world much longer, but a warm Paradise awaits. Come closer to me, O hEynne, and I will tell you what you must do."

Cautiously, as if approaching a spirit hidden in a tree trunk, Murtogh edged toward the sickly man. Indeed, he reeked of imminent death and Murtogh feared catching the fever plague from him. But the priest's words were nearly inaudible; Murtogh had to bend close, to hear.

"You must go, Murtogh O hEynne, to reclaim your cursed isle. Gather your men, your weapons, your horses and hounds, your best warriors. And prepare for war. You may kill the Spaniards, but you must start first with the origin of all this trouble: The dark maiden."

20.

Jacobo de Adamo paced the tiny confines of the priest Comgall's house, as night waned into morning. He was mightily annoyed with his son's lengthy disappearance.

"Where is he!" he roared toward Comgall, who sat at his table breakfasting on the last bones of the delectable swan.

"Let the boy alone," the priest snapped. "He's had a busy few days and is likely sleeping it all off...somewhere."

"What do you know about anything, priest?" Jacobo snarled.

Comgall glanced up briefly from his bones. Unbeknownst to Jacobo, Comgall knew the whole sorry tale of the maiden Fiona, a mere lass of fifteen who had fully expected her Spanish lover to marry her after becoming pregnant with his child. Instead, she died a long and painful death from childbed fever, after being used by this Spanish cad. If his beloved Orlaith were still alive, she would not tolerate the sight of him, she'd be chasing him from the island herself with a blazing torch. Comgall thought Jacobo had a lot of nerve showing up now to claim the abandoned boy as his own. But he felt grudgingly grateful to the Madeiran for ridding his parish isle of pirates and for the once-in-a-lifetime Easter feast. His little girl Itta had gone to sleep still clutching a whole orange tightly in her hand.

"He better bring that wench back with him," Jacobo growled. "Along with that pearl. We'll take her and the gem, then get out of here for good. Get back to Madeira, where we belong.'

"Ireland is not to your liking?"

"It is not a terrible place." Jacobo sniffed. "I've visited here often enough. But I miss my own dear house and lands. I am eager for my boy to see them. Madeira is such a beautiful isle. Still wild enough to be beautiful, yet civilized enough for comfort. There are already many good families there, it will be quite the task to figure out which one of their daughters will be best for my Aedan."

"You're planning to marry him off? But he's trained for the priesthood."

Jacobo snorted. "There are priests aplenty in Madeira. A priest son is useless to me. I need someone to carry on the name, the business. Someone to care for me in my old age. Someone who can give me grandchildren, a line."

"But he seems quite besotted with this dark girl."

Jacobo glared at him, his eyes dark with fury. Comgall dropped the bone he'd been sucking on.

"What? What did I say?"

"It's not a girl he's besotted with, priest. It's a *beast*. A mere animal, a novelty the Basques likely picked up on some primitive isle off Africa. Something they used and discarded. She would not be fit for him, a boy with education and nobility in his blood."

Comgall was taken aback. "But...I've seen her. She is a true, and quite fetching, lass. As pretty as any Irish maid, though darker—"

"She's not human, I tell you. "

"You are completely wrong, Spaniard."

"Well, she may be human, but the lowest order of humans. I have seen such wretches off Capo Verde, running about naked and dirty, eating raw meat, killing each other with abandon. In the port cities, their women work as prostitutes. But Aedan can indulge his curiosity with her, that way he gets it all out of his system before we get to Madeira, and then he must start courting young women of true quality."

"Are you taking the girl with you?"

"Of course." Jacobo shrugged. "There is a brisk trade for slaves on the Continent. Especially for exotic females. I could probably get a decent price for her on the continent before we sail off to Madeira."

"You're planning to sell her?" Comgall was horrified, at the thought of humans selling other humans. True, there had been slaves in old Eire— Saint Patrick himself had been one. But he'd thought that barbaric practice had ended centuries ago. Even more chilling was Jacobo's urbane and offhand way of discussing it, as a business transaction: As if it were no worse than selling a pair of shoes, or a basket of plums.

"That's where I'll sell the pearl, too, in Lisbon. That's the best market, among the Jews there who buy gems to sell to royalty. That pearl will finance my son's future house and farm on Madeira."

Comgall set down his chewed-out bones as Jacobo stomped out into the sunrise. The priest felt deeply unsettled. Should he warn Aedan of his father's plans? Convince him to remain in Ireland, and perhaps go to the mainland with the girl? Or would Aedan be better off with his natural father, becoming rich and prosperous on that balmy isle in the Atlantic? Was any of it *his* business?

Yes, he told himself. The boy is my family, too. He may not be of my blood, but he shares the blood of my children and their mother.

He called to his son. "Colm! Go out to the western shore, and find your cousin. Tell him to get back here at once. I must talk with him before he makes any decision about going off with his so-called father."

21.

"Aedan! Cousin! Where are you?"

In the dark of the cave overlooking the sea, Aedan awoke, spotting Colm's red hair blazing against the morning light.

"Go away," he mumbled, still sleepy, warm beneath the blanket of wool cloaks.

"You have to come now. Father says he needs to talk to you."

Marra, several feet away, now stirred. Aedan sighed heavily.

"Very well. Go tell him I am on my way. We are on our way." He now gently shook Marra awake. She turned away from him.

"Need more sleep."

"We have to get up and go, Marra. It's morning. The others are waiting for us back at the village, the church—"

"No," she murmured, sleepily. "Not go. Stay here."

"Marra, this a big day for us. We are leaving the island. You and I. We're going with my father to Madeira. See his ship out there in the water? It is better than Urraco's."

A look of terror crossed her face. "No. No ship."

"But we must leave here. We must leave Ireland." Even as he said this, he felt a terrible pang of longing and regret. How could he leave his native land, the only place he had ever known?

"We will have a good life together there, Marra. Please wake up and rise! We must go *now*." He pulled the cloaks off of her. "Think of it. We can be together now like this, every night."

She smiled. Though she and Aedan had shared only a kiss the night before, falling asleep chastely in each other's arms, it was clear this appealed to her greatly.

He went on: "We shall live together in a house. We will have our own farm, grow food, keep animals." Then, shyly, "We will have a family of our own, children..."

"Children!" At this she seemed astonished.

"But you have to get up!"

Reluctantly, she rose. He picked up Anhin's brown cloak and set it on her shoulders. Petulantly, she pulled it off again.

"Marra, please!" He firmly put the cloak back on her, but when he drew back, saw her eyes were filled with terror.

"Aedan, I fear. I afraid."

He took her hands. "No one will hurt you ever again. But you must trust me. Please?" He pulled her toward the door of the cave. "Come, Marra. Come out into the world with me."

Slowly, warily, she took his hand, and stepped outside the cave, into the brilliant, seabird-filled air.

At the steps of the church, Comgall and Jacobo de Adamo stood, waiting.

"Here they come, Aedan, and his dark sweetheart." Comgall murmured, watching as the pair made their way across the sheep meadow. "You must admit, she is quite striking, a real beauty."

"In the way that savage girls are," Jacobo muttered. "*I* wouldn't call her a beauty. To me, a woman's beauty comes from her adornments and breeding. That girl has none."

"She has a pearl." But Comgall did not turn to face Jacobo; he was watching the careful, deferential way Aedan was leading the girl across the fields.

"He is taken with her, no doubt of it," he murmured. "Your boy may not be so willing to leave Inis Ghall now."

"Nonsense. We will be leaving as planned. As soon as the damned wind picks up."

Aeden shyly approached his father and the priest, formally presenting Marra to them as if she were visiting royalty. She glanced anxiously at Aedan, then at the men, then at Aedan again.

"Don't worry," he told her soothingly. "This is my father Jacobo de Adamo. And you know the priest, Colm's father. "

"Yes," she said, quietly, in her captors tongue. "He is good man."

"She speaks the Basque!" Jacobo seemed astounded. "My mother's own tongue!"

"Yes, she learned it from the men who captured her. I told you, she is very intelligent."

177

"Look at her!" Comgall marveled. "Such eyes—magnificent! And how swarthy her skin is, as if burnt by the summer sun! Have you ever seen the likes?"

"I have," said Jacobo, dismissively, with a shrug. "She puts me in mind of the Canaries people, or those of North Africa. Except that her hair is thick and straight. But with those cheekbones...I daresay she might be Oriental, for that is how I have heard them described."

"Oriental!" Comgall was profoundly startled. "From Cathay, on the other side of the world? My word!"

"She was captured by the Basques amid an archipelago of tropical islands," Aedan explained.

"An archipelago, you say? That could be the Indies, Java and the Molluccas. Remote isles off Cathay proper. What else could it be?" Jacobo laughed. "Those crazy Basque whalers! Imagine them getting that far in their leaky carracks!"

"Marra says she came here west-to-east," Aedan pointed out. "Urraco himself told me they had sailed first to Africa, then were blown west. They took Marra and her father there, sailed north into the Arctic, then ended up here."

"Hmmm. Interesting." Jacobo rubbed his chin. "That western sea is a big place. But those pirates often lie. She is not a bad-looking wench, boy."

"Father!" Aedan murmured, embarrassed. Jacobo suddenly leaned forward and pulled at the neckline of Marra's cloak; she flinched in fear and pulled back.

Aedan was dismayed. "Father, what are you *doing*?"

"I want to see the pearl again."

"Don't be so rough with her!" Aedan motioned to Marra to show his father the gem she wore about her neck. He was still angered by his father's impolite motion. He would surely not do that to an Irish or other European woman, no matter how humble they might be.

Marra obediently dangled the golden pearl before Jacobo's eyes.

"Ahhh! It is marvelous," Jacobo murmured, his eyes gleaming. "It's stunning. It will finance an entire armada, a whole village!" He turned to Aedan. "There are surely more where that one came from."

"Perhaps," Aedan said, uneasily, motioning for Marra to hide the pearl again. "I'm more concerned with how we'll get Marra off this island. Once the islanders rise for the day and catch sight of her—"

"Oh, they can't see her!" Comgall pushed them all toward the church. "They still think she's a witch, and want her dead. Best they not see her at all."

Jacobo shrugged. "So, we will row out to the ship tonight, after dark. No one will see us go."

"Yes, but it's early morn now," said Aedan. "What will we do until then? People are bound to stop by the church, perhaps even your own quarters, uncle. And she looks like no one else on this isle. How will we keep her hidden?"

Comgall considered this. "We could try and turn her into an Irishwoman."

"And how would we do that?"

"We could start by dressing her like one. I think my late Orlaith's clothing will fit her perfectly."

In his room, he took from a trunk a new shift and head-wrap, and a gown of deep claret red, ragged at the hem. He handed this to Aedan.

"This was your mother's, once. Recognize it, Spaniard? Maybe you bought it for her, in Galway?"

Jacobo merely turned away and stomped out of doors.

"It became Orlaith's, and now…Marra's." Comgall smiled, sadly. Aedan was deeply touched. "Thank you, uncle."

"Let me go out and try to calm your father down. But Aedan, I need to speak with you seriously, at some point today."

Aedan turned to Marra and pulled the old brown cloak off her shoulders.

"Your father," she said, sadly. "No like me."

"He is in a bad mood," said Aedan, with a sigh. "He wants to be sailing, already. But he will come to like you, see what I see in you, I am sure of it."

"No ship," she said, stubbornly.

"You must take off that dirty old shift, and put this nice white one on. Wait till I turn—" But without a moment's hesitation, she stripped off her old shift, standing before him a moment completely naked but for her pearl. He tried not to look, but her bare skin glowed like her pearl.

"On my island, we wear no things. Like this," she said, with a certain pride.

"Put your shift on, please!" he cried, panicky. Then, in a gentler voice: "You'll catch cold."

She donned the cream-colored garment, which hung to her knees.

"And you really need more than a linen shift in our climate." He picked up the claret gown, and gazed at it for a moment. "My mother's. I am so honored, for you to wear it." He helped slip it over her head, over the shift, then, awkwardly, smoothed the wrinkles of the fabric along the curves of her body. It fit her perfectly, as if it had been made for her. The scarlet color was splendid with her deep-hued skin and black hair.

"Oh Marra! How beautiful you look!"

She made a face. "I not like. Heavy. Too warm."

"You must wear this now. And this, too, on your head." The linen head-wrap proved to be a true puzzle, but he did the best he could, tucking her long veil of black hair into the neck of her gown, and winding the cloth about her head and under her chin. When he was done, all that showed was a perfect oval of brown face, and her magnificent dark eyes.

Suddenly she pulled the pearl from her neck again, and re-tied it around Aedan's. The string was beginning to fray a bit, with all the handling it had undergone recently.

"You keep," she said, firmly.

"No, it's yours!"

"I want you keep. If something happen to me…"

"Nothing will happen to you!" But he left the pearl about his own neck, tucking it under the collar of his own *leine*. He would keep it safe for her during the journey they were about to take. He would not let his father sell it.

Comgall came back into the room, with the boy Colm trotting at his heels.

"She is utterly exquisite in that gown," said Comgall. "But clearly, not an Irishwoman."

Colm suddenly piped up: "You could paint her!"

Comgall moved to shoo him away, but Aedan stopped him. "Wait! That's *brilliant!*" He bent down to talk to the boy. "Can you paint her face and hands, to make her look like an Irish maiden?"

"I know just the colors to use! I'll go and get my powders."

As he ran off, Comgall turned to Aedan. "As you know, I am no stranger to the temptation of love. I know it is forbidden to me by my superiors, and yet—" He threw up his hands. "When I set eyes on my dear Orlaith, I knew I could not live without her by my side. So I understand you, my nephew. I understand your tenderness and affection for this girl. I see that it is real. But I fear, your father does not."

"I know, uncle. It's a shock to him, but he will come to accept her. He must! Especially as she learns our ways." But even as he was saying this, Marra, was tugging, yanking at the front of her gown, as if trying to rip it away from her skin. Gently, he stilled her hands.

"Far be it from me to give you advice," Comgall continued, reluctantly. "Or go against your father's wishes for you. But if you are serious about this girl, don't go with your father."

Aedan dropped his hands from Marra's, and stared at him.

"Don't get on that ship," Comgall continued, tersely. "But take her away now, immediately, off this island and into Eire. Don't even wait for the tide; take Donnacha's curragh and row across with her now—"

"But why would I do that, uncle? I know nothing of Eire save for this island and Galway. We'll have a good life in Madeira, a different life, but it will be warm, like Marra's own land. Besides," he said, with a laugh, as Colm rushed back in with his paints and powders. "I know nothing of rowing or steering a skin boat!"

Colm insisted on privacy for his artistic efforts, so Aedan and Comgall were sent outside while he went to work on Marra. Aedan heard her giggling as Colm stared his work.

Jacobo was outdoors, glowering at the sky. The eastern horizon was turning an ominous gray, while the west was already nearly black with storm clouds.

"I don't like the looks of this. We may not be setting off tonight after all."

"This is Irish weather," Aedan told him. "There'll be a storm and it will pass, probably sunny by noon again." He dropped his voice. "Father, Marra is very frightened of the ship. I hope you will try to be polite and patient with her, considering what she has been through—"

"Son," his father then said, his face almost as dark as the clouds above. "I think this has gone far enough, this game of love you're playing, with the brown wench—"

"She's no wench. And it's no game. And she will come with me when I go with you back to Madeira."

"Look, she is very interesting and exotic and attractive in her own way, but you cannot have any kind of relationship with her. Or future."

Aedan stared at him.

"You are a naïve, foolish boy, raised without women, in a place where men never spoke of them. So it's left to me to tell you these things. She's a *savage*, son. An uneducated pagan. She is meant to be a slave, maybe a servant-girl, nothing more. She may be taught language, the way a dog can be taught commands. But ultimately, she will have to be parted with, sold—"

"No. No, *NO!*" Aedan shouted. "She is not a *thing*, to be sold!"

"She's young, so she would fetch a good price in Lisbon."

"She is not for sale!" Aedan was aghast, that his father would suggest such a thing. "You are completely wrong about her! She is foreign, but of royal blood, I am sure of it. She may not be educated, as I was, but she is intelligent. And incredibly brave."

"At your age, it is easy to make fantasy, fall under Cupid's spell. You've never known other girls, what have you to compare her to? Enjoy what you can with her, but don't get too involved—"

"It is too late. I am involved with her. I am in love with her! I intend to make her my wife!"

"You fool!" Jacobo exploded. "What do you know of love? Of women? Raised by priests! You can barely talk to her, how do you expect to make a life with that wretch?"

"I will," said Aedan, stubbornly.

"Then there is no place for you on my ship, nor in my home, in Madeira!"

"Then I will not go to your damned Madeira!" Aedan shouted back, his face reddening.

Jacobo was taken aback by his son's powerful response, and softened his own tone.

"We'll discuss this later. There is too much at stake, for all to be lost in a silly quarrel. Fathers and sons fight all the time, it means nothing."

"Would you try to control me so, in Madeira? Am I to be your son, or merely under your employ?" said Aeden, coldly now.

"I'm glad to see you have a backbone, at least. I told you, we'll discuss this later."

"Maybe," said Aedan, turning from him. "Maybe not." He stalked back into Comgall's dwelling.

"Behold!" Colm greeted him. "Your fair maiden!"

Aedan gasped. Marra was no longer dark-hued, that was certain. But Colm had, with a ten-year-old's imagination, painted her up in ugly splotches of white and pink and red. She looked exactly like an old woman in the final stages of a pox.

"Cousin! She looks *dreadful*!"

"Yes! If I made her beautiful, that would attract as much attention as her being brown. This way, the islanders will work to stay clear of her."

185

Little Itta, who had been watching her brother intently, now daubed some of the paint on her own face. "Don't!" her brother scolded, wiping her cheek. "You'll give our secret away!"

"A strange genius your boy has," Aedan remarked to Comgall, who now stood by the doorway, only half-way inside. He was looking upward, with a vague look of alarm on his face.

"Do you hear that?" he asked. "Aedan, do you hear something?"

"Hear what?"

"A sort of vibration, or soft roar—"

"Probably thunder, from the coming storm."

"No. I can *feel* this..." He placed his hand on the door frame.

Jacobo suddenly appeared alongside the priest. "Come," he said, with a look of apprehension on his face.

They all moved outdoors, the two men, Aedan, Marra and Colm, carrying his little sister. The storm had not started yet, and they hurried down toward the strait separating the island from the mainland. There they watched, their mouths falling open, as a huge army of Irish warriors on horseback, accompanied by hundreds of barking hounds, thundered swiftly across the ebb-tide path toward Inis Ghall.

22.

Murtogh O hEynne now swung down off his white steed, and walked purposefully toward the priest Comgall, who could only stare wide-eyed at the burly, bearded man in the ill-fitting gold-velvet waistcoat, a huge, primitive centuries-old hatchet hanging from his belt.   He had only seen the chieftain a few times in the past, on the mainland and never actually on this island of his.

"Sire, what brings you to Inis Ghall?" he asked, nervously. Marra, meanwhile, swiftly dashed back inside Comgall's hut with the children, while Aedan and Jacobo stayed put.

"I hear there's some trouble going round this island," said Murtogh in a growling, irritated way.

"Oh. No, there is no trouble. Not anymore. It's true, we had a bit of a fever here, but it seems to be dying out."

"I'm not talking about a fever! I'm talking about that damned Spanish ship off the west coast out there!"

"That? 'Tis only a visitor, sir. It is — "

Aedan's father strolled forward, extending his hand. "Jacobo de Adamo, wine merchant of

Madeira, Lisbon and Castille. I am only here to retrieve something I lost, good sir."

Murtogh raised his eyebrows and did not accept the hand extended to him. "Your Irish is not half bad," he muttered, grudgingly. But a heavy tension hung in the air, as well as heavy air signaling the impending storm. Aedan, waiting to see what would happen between his father and the Irish chieftain, found his eyes drawn toward the mainland. He saw, struggling along the tidal path across the strait, two men—one walking, wearing an ankle-length black cloak, the other a hooded cripple in finer cloth, thrown across the back of a donkey like a sack of grain. He suddenly recognized the hatless, bald shining pate of Brother Paulus of St. Alban's, and yelped in sheer astonishment, running toward the men.

"Brother Paulus!" he cried as he ran, running halfway toward the mainland where he met the two men and their donkey in the very middle. Paulus pulled aside the hood of the invalid man, revealing the skeletal and barely conscious Lord Fulke.

"My lord!" Aedan gasped. "What are you—Why are you *here*, of all places!" Swiftly, he pulled the near-comatose man from the donkey, holding him in his arms like a child. He was stunned at how little his teacher weighed, and the awful sallowness of his skin, the orbs of his eyes.

"He insisted on coming," said Paulus, mournfully. "To see you."

"Aedan," the priest Fulke whispered, before shutting his eyes against the cloud-choked sky.

Aedan struggled back to Ghall with Fulke in his arms, Paulus and the beast gamely following behind.

Back at the church steps, Murtogh and Jacobo were now laughing and clapping each other on the shoulder. My father, thought Aedan fleetingly, could charm a snake.

Jacobo glanced at the man in Aedan's arms. "Ah, there he is. The pathetic clerical wretch who invented such tales about me!"

"Father!" Aedan cried, still holding Fulke, "Can you not have some respect for the man who raised me?"

"That man caused us quite a bit of trouble," Murtogh snapped. "Trying to convince us the end of the world was nigh! Invasions by Spaniards, indeed!" He turned to Jacobo. "Let's see that hand-cannon of yours."

Aedan brushed past them and into the dwelling room of Father Comgall. Marra, in her guise of diseased Irish hag, looked up in surprise. She was sitting with Colm and Itta, feeding them circles of carrots she had sliced with Comgall's blade. They in turn were teaching her Irish words—*cairéad*, carrot and *scian*, knife. Aedan placed Fulke on the pallet of sleeping hay, then turned to his cousins.

"My father is going to shoot his cannon again," he told them and they gleefully ran back outdoors. He then turned to Marra.

"This is my Lord Fulke. A good man, the man who was a real father to me..." For emphasis, he gently patted the priest's head. "He will only rest here, and not hurt you. Don't be afraid of him."

She seemed to understand him fully, nodded sympathetically before returning to the oak table to resume cutting carrots and turnips for a pot she had set on the fire. But she did glance over at the man asleep in the hay with wary, watchful eyes.

Aedan then went back outdoors. He wanted to make sure the O hEynne clan was briefly entertained and then sent on their way. He did not know if the mainland men presented a threat to Marra or not, but he did not want to run the risk of finding out.

And he was dreading the conversation he would have to have with Lord Fulke, when the priest awoke from his rest. Aedan knew he would have to be truthful with his mentor and strong, too. He knew Fulke would use his best arguments to try to persuade Aedan to return to St. Alban's and leave Marra behind. That was the only reason Fulke had made this arduous journey, only to retrieve him. Aedan did not have the heart to tell him his mission had been in vain.

Down at the waterfront facing the mainland, Jacobo was adjusting the plank board that supported his little cannon. Comgall watched dolefully as his children darted about excitedly, and he labored to keep them as far from the weapon as possible. Murtogh seemed almost as excited as the little ones, eager to see the handgun show its work. Darkening clouds continued knitting themselves together overhead and the wind grew brisk.

"This will change the entire course of warfare," Jacobo was saying cheerfully. "Would you like to try it, Sir Murtogh?"

"I would indeed!"

"Now you can imagine you are invading the Irish mainland," said Jacobo with a chuckle. "Be sure the gun is supported on this board, elsewise the force will knock you over. First, we load the barrel with gunpowder."

"A secret recipe, is it not? From the Orient?"

"Hah! No secret to it, only saltpeter, charcoal and sulfur. You can find all that in Ireland."

"Is this what the warriors of Europe are using now?" Murtogh wanted to know.

"Not so much in Europe as in Asia Minor. The Turks especially are quite skilled in their use. They have gigantic gun barrels capable of bringing down city walls. Now—this hempen rope is arranged to set it off." He turned to a small iron pot which contained a glowing ember.

"You're not going to damage my property, are you?" asked Murtogh with some concern.

"No, no, my good man. I'm not loading it with anything but powder. It'll make a splendid bang and nothing else!" Jacobo ceremoniously handed iron tongs containing the glowing ember to Murtogh. "My lord, if you please. Just hold the hot ember to the hemp. And stand back—"

Murtogh gingerly lifted the red-hot coal to the touchhole and suddenly there was a flash of yellow light, a hellish explosion and much blue smoke, followed by much hooting and applause by the Irishmen.

An exasperated Brother Paulus, who had just been leading his donkey onto dry land from the strait, now scurried off after the terrified beast, who had taken off like a bolt.

"What a grand thing!" Murtogh crowed. "Can we do it again?"

"Well, perhaps a few times more, before the rain comes." Jacobo looked up at the sky, then at the embers pot. "It seems I need some more embers. I'll just go inside to the church's kitchen hearth and retrieve a few more."

When he left, Aedan sidled up to Comgall. "Do you think the O hEynne will leave soon?"

"I doubt it. They brought tents and such, and they seem to be setting up in the sheep meadow. At least your father has charmed them and calmed them down. Where did those brats of mine get off to?"

Aedan watched unhappily as Murtogh intently inspected the iron cannon, gingerly touching its hot surface. He suddenly turned to Aedan.

"So! You're the boyo the priest was looking for? You've caused quite a bit of commotion round here."

"I'm sorry for that, sir."

"That your father in there, the Spaniard?"

"Yes, sir."

Murogh winked at him. "You'll have an easier life if you go off with him, and not back to the priests. Not that life is all about money, but it does make things easier for a man, if he has it."

Suddenly a shout came from the direction of the church. It was Jacobo, running and shouting something frantically, in Basque, to Aedan. Something about blood, a murder...

Aedan felt his blood run cold. *Marra! Please Lord, not Marra!* He ran toward the room where he had left her with Fulke and rushed in—

There stood Marra with a pained, confused look on her painted face. In her hand, the carrot-chopping knife dripped with blood. On the earthen floor at her feet lay Lord Fulke, blood pumping from a wound in his chest.

Aedan did not even have time to speak, or reach out for her. Jacobo and Comgall and Murtogh and the whole of his army were pressing in on him, filling the room.

"I told you," said Jacobo, flushed, but now calm, cold. "She is a *savage*. She does not know right from wrong."

"She did not do this!" Aedan cried. "She could not have!"

"Take her," said Murtogh to his men. "Take the woman outside and tie her to the stake."

"No, no, please, don't kill her!" Aedan struggled to reason with him, as his men yanked Marra away and out of the room, out into a now raging rainstorm. "Please, there must be some other explanation, someone else must have been in here—" But Murtogh and his men grimly pushed him aside, dragging the girl to the stake, tying her to it, struggling with her as sheets of rain poured down and the wind howled about.

"Please don't kill her!" Aedan begged. "Let her explain!"

But suddenly, the Irishmen, the islanders, began to shout in horror and alarm. The pouring rain was now washing away the pink, red and white paint from Marra's face, revealing the bronzed skin underneath. Murtogh yanked at the linen headdress and her black hair poured out. For a stunned moment, he stared at her unfamiliar features, and her darkness.

"Aha," he murmured. "The black witch shows herself at last."

23.

By early evening, the storm had abated and clear skies covered Inis Ghall.   The O hEynne clan had set up camp for the night on the sheep fields beyond the church, but two men were left to guard the 'witch' tied to the stake.

Marra, wet and cold, still in her gown of claret, sat slumped at the base of the stake, her hands tied behind it; she seemed oblivious to the cold and wet, the prickly base of twigs and thorny brush beneath her. Her Irish guards would not let Aedan get near her, so he tried to catch her attention from beyond, calling to her. She did not respond, not even with a glance in his direction.

Defying the guards, he darted forward and grabbed at her shoulder.

"Marra! Look at me! Just tell me, yes or no. Did you kill my Lord Fulke?"

But she would not look him, nor would she answer.

"Yes, or no? Did you kill him? Tell me!"

The guards now swatted roughly at him, and pulled him away. "Get out of here, pest. Else you'll be burned with her on the morrow."

Numb with grief and fear, he stumbled back into the church, where Brother Paulus was preparing Fulke's body for its return to Galway, wrapping it in strips of linen for the boat journey back.

"Aedan, this is a most terrible thing that had come to pass. A murder. And now our church has no leader."

"I know," Aedan whispered.

"If that girl is indeed responsible, she must pay the price. Lord Fulke was a great man."

Aedan hung his head. "Brother Paulus, I do not believe she did this to him."

"Who, then? She was holding the knife. No one else was there."

"I can't believe she would hurt anyone let alone commit murder."

The older man studied him thoughtfully.

"What is your tie to this girl?"

"I planned to make her my wife. I wanted to have a life with her."

"And yet you know nothing about her. She is a foreigner, a pagan. Not one of us." He placed a hand on Aedan's shoulder. "You're the lamb who's wandered away from the flock. Come back with me now, boy, to Galway city. Forget this sordid isle. The lass will die whether she's guilty or innocent; you know the O hEynne will not let her go. Come and take up your student's robe again, and the Almighty will forgive all transgressions."

Aedan felt sick and weary with grief, full of confusion. He thought with some longing of his little cell at St. Alban's, the richly stocked library with its maps...

"No," he murmured. "I cannot. I must stay, and see this all through. I must try to find out what really happened. I must know the truth. Otherwise, my life at St. Alban's would be full of bitterness and confusion."

"You will not come back even to see your foster-father laid to rest?" Paulus asked, his words filled with reprimand and sorrow.

"I cannot. I will pray for his soul, and mourn the terrible way he left this earth. But I cannot return to St. Alban's, not now."

Murtogh's men came to help Paulus place Fulke's body into a small boat for the crossing to the mainland, for the tide was in. There they would be met by a contingent of men who would accompany Paulus and the corpse back to Galway. Aedan stood at the strait and watched as they rowed away. Under his linen shirt, he fingered the outline of the pearl Marra had given him. It felt cold and hard against his own skin.

"Come back to us, Aedan." Paulus called out to him. "Come back, when all is over…"

Aedan turned and trudged inside his uncle's dwelling, wanting to confront his father. Jacobo had been the only witness to the alleged crime, and he was being curiously close-mouthed about the whole affair.

"I want you to tell me exactly what you saw. I want to know every detail," Aedan demanded.

Jacobo would not look his son in the eye. "I told you, I came in to retrieve some live coals. I saw what you saw, the girl holding the bloody knife. Fulke there on the floor, dead."

"You did not actually see her kill him."

"I did not have to. I understood what happened clearly enough."

Aedan stared at the dark indigo-blue of Jacobo's doublet. There seemed some darkish stain about the front lacing.

"Is that blood there, on your doublet?" he asked. Jacobo shrugged.

"I suppose the girl brushed the knife against me. I grabbed her as soon as I saw what she had done."

"Why would Marra kill my Lord Fulke? It makes no sense."

"Does she need a reason? Do savages and madwomen need reasons for their actions? Only she knows, son. She and your poor Lord Fulke. Perhaps he provoked her in some way."

"No! He was asleep when I left him. And almost near death then. "

"He would have died anyway. So it is not such a great matter, is it?"

Aedan was shocked. "It is, if he was murdered!"

"Come with me now," said Jacobo, suddenly. "Your girl, her fate is sealed. She will be killed by the Irish in the morning. Do you really want to be around to see that? They will no doubt torture her first. Then she'll be set ablaze. You can't want to watch that. Come with me now, we'll row out to the ship this instant. At dawn we will be sailing south of here. First to Limerick, then on to Lisbon and Madeira."

Aedan merely stared at him, unable to respond.

"I take it you managed to get the pearl," Jacobo added.

"Why would you assume that?"

"Because the girl wasn't wearing it—"

"—when she supposedly killed Lord Fulke?" Aedan finished his sentence. "How would you know that, Father?"

"All right, I did try to take her pearl, in the moments after the stabbing because...I knew once the Irish had apprehended her for the murder, well, I couldn't let such a precious gem fall into their hands, could I? Idiot Irish clans! They're practically as savage as she is! They wouldn't know what to do with it!" He gave Aedan a worried look. "You do have it, don't you, son?"

"I have it," Aedan said, coldly. A look of relief spread across Jacobo's face.

"Well, then. What's to detain us? Let's go."

"No.

"Son—"

"I said no. I won't go. Not now. Not tonight. I'm not going with you."

"I am your father!" Jacobo shouted. "I am all you have left now!"

Aedan stared at the man he felt he no longer knew. With his nose and chin, his facial features so much like Aedan's own, whose very blood flowed in Aedan's own veins: Could *he* have been the one to send that blade into Lord Fulke's chest? Could he be capable of such a monstrous crime? It seemed utterly absurd to Aedan, impossible. Jacobo was an urbane, intelligent man, with a distaste for blood. He could not believe his father capable of such an action. And then, to lie about it...

"Look, we must go now," Jacobo continued, brusquely. "The storm is over, and the winds are favorable."

"What's the hurry?" Aedan snapped. "Your ship will still be there tomorrow. Madeira will still be out there in the western sea, waiting for you. I tell you, I will go nowhere until the morning."

Jacobo's face reddened, but he did not respond. Ever the businessman, the negotiator...Aedan could see that Jacobo was trying, even now, to smooth this matter over, pull Aedan back over to his side, win him back. But what did his father truly want? Aedan, his son...or that wretched pearl?

Aedan turned and walked back into the night, toward the stake where Marra was tied. The guards made menacing gestures toward him, so he hid himself in shadows a short distance away, so he could watch over her and make sure no harm came to her, in the night.

24.

Marra stared at the Irish night sky, waiting for death with a strange sort of calm. She knew now the pale men intended to kill her in the morning, that's why they had tied her here, atop the pile of dry brush and sticks. They would roast her, like the terrible *Caribe* tribe from her home islands might, and then maybe, as those Caribe would, eat her parts, to gain her wisdom and strength.

She could escape. She could easily unpick the feeble knots they used to bind her. But she didn't want to run and hide anymore in this strange land, and be hunted again like an animal. She merely wanted it all to be over: In death, she would be reunited with her ancestors, her mother and her father. There would be no more running, hiding, fearing. No more cold, cold sea.

But as the evening progressed and the moon hung shining in the sky, a damp chill infecting the night air, she began to have doubts about what awaited her in the afterlife. What would her mother and father say to her, in the other world? Would they scold her, for not putting up more of a fight? Would they be angry with her, ashamed, calling her weak? Might they say, *Go away! You are too*

young to be here with us! You have not yet had children.
Go back to earth, to the golden-haired one the gods have
selected for you.

Aedan: She could not forget the look on his face, the anguish and fear. How could she tell him the hard, bitter truth of it all? How could she ever explain it to him, with her imperfect words, something she did not even understand herself?

Everything happened in an eye-blink, a flash of lightning. The storm, the mainland tribes invading, the sick man, the knife...

First came the storm, so violent and sudden, sheets of rain, gusts of wind so strong she felt the thatched roof of the little hut groan and creak above her. She feared a *hurri-cano* was coming, one of those frightful storms that plagued her islands in the late summer and fall. It was spring here, but everything was different, in this world.

The paint the boy had laid on her face felt thick, crusted, on her skin; the garments itched and strafed her. She had been terrified by the arrival of even more strange men on the island, those mainlanders riding their fearsome beasts across the path in the sea. She had never seen horses before. But she knew what the arrival of those men meant: War. They may not have been painted as the *Caribe* adorned themselves for battle, but they shouted and cried out as those warriors did. She understood an invasion when she saw one.

And wars, battles, she knew, brought nothing but grief and sorrow to those who did not fight. Men, women and children would all be killed.

She did not know what the battle was about, but feared it might have something to do with her, her presence on the island. She wanted to flee, but felt trapped in folds of fabric, the thick mask Colm had painted on her. She took little comfort in the fact that she was disguised. More people might die, because of her. Perhaps her own beloved Aedan. She regretted bitterly that they had not fled the island together sooner.

She continued to occupy herself by cutting the root vegetables with Comgall's kitchen blade, sliding the circle shapes into a kettle that boiled on the coals. She felt uneasy with the shiny metal blade: It was sharper than any flint knife she had ever used, too slippery, and she feared cutting her own fingers. Then Koe-lum and his sister came to join her, and for a while they sat together, while the children told her Irish words for things, and she fed them bits of carrot. The little girl Itta had put a tiny finger on Marra's painted hand, then scraped away the flaky paint with her fingernail, beaming at Marra as if they were sharing a private joke.

Aedan came in with the sick man. She saw that he was quite distraught, near tears, because of this man. She watched as he gently touched the man's head. This was a man precious to Aedan, more precious than his own black-bearded father. She then remembered he had spoken of having another father, the man who raised him. She was moved by the tenderness Aedan showed this man.

When Aeden left with the children, she went to look at the man. He stared up at her with hollow eyes. His face was sallow with illness, and his mouth seemed desert-dry, moving but unable to issue words. She saw he was about to die.

She brought a bowl of fresh water over to the sick man and, using a wooden spoon, carefully dropped the clear, cool liquid into his mouth. He sipped it gratefully. She then dipped the tail end of her headwrap into the water and dabbed his fevered brow. It was as hot as a sunbaked rock.

He gazed up her, unfazed by her strange painted appearance. He did not seem to fear her. She cocked her head, as he moved his mouth to speak. Only one strange sound emerged. To her ears it sounded like *aaaan-jellll*. Anjel? But she had little time to ponder this mystery, for suddenly the man Jak-ko-bo, Aedan's father, blew in.

He frightened her, this man who had sired Aedan. Even though she could see Aedan's features in his, the same straight nose and chin, he was very different from his son. He was big man, darker than his son, but this did not make him handsome to her. There seemed a coldness in him, perhaps the kind of hardness that seeps into older men everywhere, men who have lived too much or too long. She cowered by the invalid, as Jacobo moved toward the hearth with fire-tongs. But swiftly, he turned to her, with a look of amusement on his face.

She had seen that look before, on the faces of her captors, on the ship.

He came at her. He called her, *puta*. Bad woman, bad girl. He pulled up the skirt of her gown, and she tried to pull away from him, but he was strong, stronger than she—

She lunged for the slicing knife on the table. She did not want to kill Aedan's father, only scare him away, make him leave. To be attacked and raped, by the father of the boy she loved—it was too horrible. She could not let it happen.

She squirmed and spun about, the knife in her hand. The man tried to grab for it.

And then the invalid rose. Like a man rising from the dead, the skeleton-man lurched toward Jacobo, feebly attempting to pull him from Marra. The Spaniard swiftly grabbed Marra's wrist and plunged her hand toward the invalid's chest. The knife, undulled even by so many carrots and roots, sliced into flesh. Blood spurted in a fountain toward her. She screamed...

Now in the dark, tied to the stake, she forced herself to review the scene over and over again. The dark-beard shouting for the others and the sick man falling, his blood draining from him, into the earthen floor. The knife was still in her hand; she had been too stunned to drop it. And Aedan saw it all.

The look on his face! That Aedan thought even for a moment she could do such a thing, to a man he cared so deeply for...it was too painful. She had no words to tell him, to explain. How could she tell him, his own father had been responsible? Would he believe her?

I have lost him, she thought, and the emptiness, the sorrow she felt was unbearable. She almost welcomed the idea of death. Far easier, she thought, to face flames or blade, than the shocked, wounded look in her love's sea-blue eyes.

As night deepened, she ran her mind relentlessly over every detail, feeling as if she had forgotten something, something significant. The hearth, the boiling kettle, the rough-hewn table where the meals were prepared and eaten...and under the table, a foot sticking out. A small foot. Not the girl's.

The boy's. Koe-lum.

The boy had been there, hiding. The boy had seen all of it. Terrified, he must have run off, horrified at the ways of adults. But the boy could save her.

It was so late now, so dark, and all were asleep, even the men assigned to watch her. Where would the boy be now? Asleep in his father's house or out wandering? She knew he liked to wander at all hours.

"Koe-lum. Koe-lum!" she called out in a low voice, into the night air. "Koe-lum," she crooned, her owl-like cries sliding into the night, each cry a bit louder than the others. The sleeping guards stirred but did not awaken.

Suddenly there was a rustle in the nearby bushes, someone approaching. It was not a guard or Koe-lum himself, but Aedan, He knelt close to her, his face close to hers.

"Marra! What is it?"

"Koe-lum," she said to him, with as much emphasis as she could. "The boy. Go! Get him."

He stared dumbly at her for what seemed minutes, then a vague light seem to come into his face. He rose and within moments returned, actually carrying the boy in his arms. Colm rubbed the sleep from his eyes.

In her desperation, she began to talk quickly with the boy in her own tongue, from her native island: *Boy! Tell Aedan what you know, what you saw, tell the truth —*

Both Aedan and Colm started at her strange words, sharing confused looks. She struggled to compose herself. She had to use the pale-men's language.

"Koe-lum. Tell Aedan. You see. Truth."

She forgot the boy spoke his own language of Ireland, not Basque. To her dismay, he suddenly bolted off, without any sign he had understood her. He ran not in the direction of the church, where he had been asleep, but off into the darkness, off toward the sheep meadow and western edge of the island.

But Aedan had understood. He glanced at Marra, his face suffused with hope, and ran off immediately after the child, disappearing into the cool Irish night.

25.

Aedan chased Colm into the darkness, catching up with him all the way down by the thundering night surf. He grabbed the struggling child against his chest, holding him until he stopped squirming.

"Tell me what you have to tell me!" Aedan demanded.

"There is nothing!" Colm cried, his voice laden with cold fright.

"What are you afraid of?"

"Your father," said the boy, in a small voice. "My father. The O hEynne."

"You're not afraid of Marra, are you?"

"No," said the boy mournfully. "I don't want her to die. But who will believe me? My father will just say I am lying."

"Just tell me the truth. What did you see when Lord Fulke was killed?"

Colm did not answer. Aedan squeezed him more tightly. "Did you see Marra kill Lord Fulke with the knife?"

"Yes!" Colm gasped, starting to cry. "But your father made her do it!"

Shocked, Aeden let the boy fall from his arms.

"She did not mean to stab Lord Fulke. He had been lying there in the hay, just sleeping. Your father came in to get some coals. I followed him inside, because I was still hungry. I wanted more pieces of carrot from Marra. But when he started to yell and beat Marra, I ran under the table."

"My father was *beating* Marra?"

"He pulled up her dress and was trying to throw her on the floor. I couldn't understand what he was saying, but he seemed angry."

Aedan felt an iciness creep into his heart.

"Marra had the knife in her hand. I think she was trying to scare him away. But then the sick man rose up from the hay and went toward them both—" He stopped to mimic the staggering gait of a deeply ill man. "He went toward your father. He said something to him, a single word. Not an Irish word. I didn't know the meaning of it. I think it was...*English*."

"What did it sound like, this word?"

"Stupp, or *sta-aw-pp*."

"*Stop*," Aedan whispered. He understood. Fulke, despite his great illness had tried, however feebly, to intervene. To help Marra. Ironically, he would not have known it was Marra, only a woman with mottled white-red skin, but in great distress. Somehow, at the end, despite the state of his body and mind, his last act was an act of charity, an urge to help another being.

"Your father then pushed Marra's arm toward Lord Fulke, and the blade went right into his chest."

Aedan moaned. He now saw, with utter clarity, the true nature of three people so dear to him: His beloved teacher, his poor Marra, only trying to defend herself, and his biological father, who had now shown himself to be a ruthless, thieving and violent knave. A man who had something to gain by removing both Lord Fulke, and Marra, from Aedan's life.

"Thank you, cousin," he whispered, embracing the boy. "Now I must go and save Marra. Get her released, somehow."

"The O hEynne, they'll never let her go!"

"We shall see."

Dawn still lay hours away. At the stake in front of the church, Marra had fallen into a twisted, uneasy state of slumber. Aedan gently touched her face.

"I will have you freed soon, my love, *mo rún*," he whispered to her. She twitched slightly, but did not awaken.

Both Jacobo and Father Comgall came striding out of the church. Comgall moved to angrily grab at his son Colm, but Aedan stilled his hand.

"Don't scold him, uncle. He has done me a great favor. He told me the truth about the murder." He turned coldly to his father. "I know what really happened with you and Marra and Lord Fulke."

"She murdered him," Jacobo said, coolly, in Irish. He shrugged. "There is nothing more to it. Are you going to believe some dirty brat's wild story? Or your own father?"

"It wasn't a lie!" Colm cried, in protest, to his own father. "This time I told the truth, not a story."

Aedan seized his father by the arm roughly and pulled him away from the others.

"Go!" he ordered Jacobo. "Go now and tell the O hEynne what you did."

In response, Jacobo suddenly slapped him, so hard Aedan nearly fell over.

"How dare you talk to me that way!"

"Tell the truth, you lying knave!" Aedan shouted back. "You tried to rape Marra! You pushed her hand toward my Lord Fulke!"

Jacobo now pursed his lips. "I hadn't wanted to tell you this, boy. But you should hear it. But I came upon the girl in the kitchen, trying to seduce your teacher, climbing into his pallet with him—"

"Stop! Stop lying!"

"When he protested, she slew him, and then attempted to seduce me as well—"

Aedan clapped his hands over his ears. "I won't hear this! Get away from me! Go back to your ship! Go back to your paradise. But I will not go with you. I want nothing to do with you."

Jacobo stared at him for a long moment. Astonishment, indignation then cold anger all flashed across his face.

"You speak as if you are not my son."

"I am not your son!" Aedan cried, in Irish. "You are not my father! You killed my father!!!"

Without another word, Jacobo turned and stalked away.

Comgall had been watching the scene, his mouth agape.

"Dear Aedan, I never quite had the courage to tell you: But I prayed you would not go with that man."

"You did?"

"He treated Fiona, your own mother, so badly. He wanted to sell your Marra as a slave! He is not a good man."

"I know that now. "

"So your girl is innocent."

"Do you think the O hEynne will free her? Is Murtogh a reasonable man?"

"Perhaps. I don't know him well at all. But he strikes me as the sort of man you could talk to, and he would listen. Up to a point. I wouldn't disturb him now so close to dawn."

"I can't wait for morning! I must free her tonight!"

"Even if he lets her go free, the islanders may come for her. They still hold her responsible for that illness, and the pirates."

"I'll take her off this island."

"You're leaving with her?"

"Yes," said Aedan, softly. "She is my life now. My life as a student in Galway is over. My life as son of Jacobo de Adamo is over. I cannot stay here with Marra. I must take her and forge a new life somewhere else in Eire…but it must be with her."

"A pity," said Comgall, sadly, "for I had come to care for you greatly, as had my children. I selfishly hoped you might stay here, with us."

Aedan embraced him. "You are the only real family I have ever known, you and my little cousins. I will come back one day, to see them grown." He let the priest go. "I do have a favor to ask, since there is a chance this is goodbye for good. It's about your son, Colm."

"You're not taking him with you, are you?"

"No, no...But I wish you would send him to Galway, to St. Alban's, for an education. Tell the priests there he is to take my place. They will accept him. I think he's very bright and this island will grow too small for him. Ask the brother, Paulus, to look after him, and to teach him art. Perhaps they will not grieve my absence so keenly, if they have another boy to watch over and teach." He turned to leave, but Comgall caught his arm.

"If Murtogh releases Marra, and the tide has not gone out...Take Donnacha's old curragh, if you need to to get to the mainland."

"And where do I go from there?"

"I don't know," said the priest, in a sinking voice. "Connemarra is a vast and mysterious wilderness, full of unpredictable clans. You will have to make your own way there."

Aeden went straight to the sheep meadow encampment, and asked the guards there to let him into the camp proper. But not without some trepidation: While Murtogh struck him as a somewhat reasonable man, he was still formidable, an enigma to Aedan. The chieftain seemed to have a secret, simmering temper hiding beneath his salt-and-pepper beard. Murtogh might be fair, but he also might be unfair, capricious, whimsical or downright ornery. He could decide to kill Marra — and Aedan — simply because he was in a bad mood.

"I need to see the O hEynne, Murtogh himself!" Aedan demanded of the man guarding the big man's tent. The guard shoved him away in annoyance.

"Get lost, boy! He's not ready to wake up yet!"

"It's urgent! I must see him at once!"

"Let him in," came a voice growling from inside the tent.

Murtogh, as it turned out, was not sleeping, but sitting up, puzzling over a primitive chessboard, alone, without an opponent, in the wan light of a flickering grease-lamp. He looked at Aedan in surprise.

"The Spaniard's son, is it?"

"Yes, sir. Aedan." He left off the surname, *de Adamo*.

"Do you know chess, boy?"

"No." It was a lie; Aedan had been a skillful player back at the abbey, where the game was much loved. But he did not want to do anything to risk incurring Murtogh's annoyance or wrath.

"Sir, I need to talk to you, about the girl Marra. "

"Ah. Your sweetheart, is she? Is it the dark skin you're liking, or does she have special powers?"

Aedan struggled not to look flustered. "No. I am betrothed to her, and plan to make her my wife."

Murtogh raised his eyebrows. "You're an adventurous one. Wouldn't you be afraid of her, that she might change herself into a raven or seal and disappear with your children?"

"No, sir. She is only a mere lass. Just darker than others."

"I see. Who is she then, and where does she come from?"

"I cannot tell you for certain, only that it is an island in the Western Sea, far to the west."

"Not Thule or the Green-land?"

"No, a warm land on the latitudes of Araby and the Mediterranean. A ship full of Basque and Spanish fishermen became marooned on the far edges of the Western Sea, and came upon her and her father by chance. They killed her father, and treated her most cruelly. When their boat foundered in a storm on the way back to Europe, they ended up here, off Eire. She jumped from the ship and swam to Inis Ghall."

"She told you all this?"

"Yes, she had learned some Basque on the ship, which, as it happens, I can understand."

"Remarkable."

"The Basques then came to Inis Ghall to look for her. They wreaked havoc before they left, burning some of the islanders' homes. It was they who brought the fever that killed so many. Not only that, but they murdered their own captain while here on the island. My father then came, and drove them off."

"Stupid knaves. So why is your father here?"

"To take me back to Madeira with him. I am his only child, his heir."

"So why are you not wanting to go back with him, boy?"

Aedan leaned forward, urgently. "Please let the girl go. She did not kill Lord Fulke."

"But they say she has. Your own father was witness."

"No. My father, the Spaniard de Adamo, forced himself on her, she picked up a knife to defend herself, but the blade met Lord Fulke instead. My father actually forced her hand in that direction.

215

There is another witness, the small boy named Colm—"

"Little boys are known to tell tales."

"My father had reason to want Lord Fulke dead. He felt my lord was keeping me from going to Madeira with him. I understand my father quarreled with Lord Fulke just before coming here."

"All very interesting, but what has this to do with anything?"

"The girl is clearly innocent, a victim. Please release her, and don't have her burned."

Murtogh stared dolefully at him across the chessboard.

"Ah...can't do it, my boy."

"But...but she did not mean to kill Lord Fulke! There is a witness!"

"Whether she killed the priest or not, it doesn't matter. It means nothing to me, who killed whom. I am the chieftain of this muddy isle, and have to maintain order. The islanders are panicked. They think she's a supernatural spirit, the devil's lass. The only way to calm them is to kill the poor girleen. Ugly business, but that's the way of our world here. I've killed men for lesser reasons. If this brings calm and peace to Ghall, then so be it."

Aedan was horrified by this explanation. "This is wrong! It's...it's un-Christian! Are you a pagan, or a believer in the true God?"

"Don't preach to me, boy! I attend the Mass on Christmas and Easter, but that's as far as it goes. I'm not a pagan, but I have my own rules, not

Rome's, based on common sense and the way things really work around here."

"Very well," said Aedan, seeing he could not appeal to Murtogh's Christianity or good sense. He decided to try a new tactic. "If it's the islanders you're worried about, what if the girl were to simply ...disappear?"

Murtogh raised an eyebrow. "Has she the power to do that?" he asked, half in jest.

"Of course not!" Aedan could barely contain his impatience. "If she were a witch or sprite, don't you think she would have freed herself by now?"

"What are you saying, boy?"

"I'm saying, I could spirit her off the island now, before dawn, before anyone notices she's gone."

"The tide is high."

"I have a boat. A curragh."

"No," said Murtogh, with a shrug.

"Why not?"

"I have to kill her, boy."

"*Why?*"

Murtogh leaned in close. "Listen to me! I am a man of almost fifty now. I have gray hairs in my beard and on my head. My men...They see that I am getting old; they make fun of me, when I get forgetful. They think I'm getting slow, soft in the head. To make things worse, I have no sons! Ten damned expensive daughters, and no males. Believe me, that does nothing to convince the others of my manliness! I cannot be making decisions and then suddenly reversing them. They'll say, the O hEynne is growing feeble, idiotic!

He let the dark witch go and why? Because some stripling boy talked him out of it!"

"Ten daughters," Aedan murmured. "That's a big outlay, for dowries."

"You don't have to tell me."

"What if I could aid you in that matter? In return, of course, for the girl's freedom?"

"Hah!" A short, explosive, bitter laugh. "A poor scholar, you! How could you help me, financially?" He raised his eyebrows. "Are you planning to shake down that rich father of yours? Blackmail?"

"No. I have a gem the girl gave me. It's the reason the Basques came here, to look for her. My father says it's worth a fortune."

"Oh, the golden pearl?"

"You heard about it?"

"The Spaniard mentioned it. He was looking for it, but it wasn't on the girl when we captured her. Do you have it?"

"Yes," said Aedan, carefully.

"So what would stop me from seizing you, taking the pearl and burning you and your girlfriend on the stake?" asked Murtogh, but with a playful sort of grin.

"You would not kill one of your own. Remember, I was born on Inis Ghall, of an Irish maiden. The priest Comgall is my uncle, his children my cousins. I am one of your charges now, and you have a duty to protect me, not injure, rob or kill me!"

"All right, let's see that pearl."

Aedan reached into the neck of his linen *leine* and pulled the gem from his neck. In the flickering light of the grease-lamp, it glowed amber-gold, like a wondrous sort of hazelnut in the palm of his hand. Murtogh seemed impressed, his eyes lighting up, but Aedan closed his fist around it before the chieftain could pluck it from his palm.

"Release her," Aedan demanded, "and the pearl is yours."

In response, Murtogh pulled a small dagger from his belt. It glinted, catching the fire flame of the grease-lamp. For a terrified second, Aedan thought he had lost everything: The pearl, Marra, perhaps his own life. But then Murtogh carelessly slid the blade across his chessboard.

"Release her yourself! The guards will be sleeping now. Then get her out of here! I don't want to know anything about it! Get that girl off this island before the dawn breaks, or I cannot say what will happen to her. Or you."

Aedan then slid the pearl over to Murtogh's side of the board. He felt a bit reluctant to let it go, knowing it was all Marra had, of her island home. But now it would gain her freedom, and her life.

Murtogh smiled at the gem for a moment, then abruptly slid it back toward Aedan.

"Thanks, boyo. A nice trifle, but you'll be needing it more than me. Now go and get out, before the rest of my men awaken. I'll have to think of something to tell them all, in the morning."

Aedan ran to the stake which held Marra tightly, just as the sky was beginning to show a hint of the coming dawn. The guards beside her were fast asleep, so his work was easy. He slid Murtogh's dagger blade through the twine in one motion, then tossed the blade aside. She awoke in surprise, as he pulled her to her feet. He half-carried her away from the guards and the church, hurrying her down to the shore of the strait, as she struggled to comprehend what was happening.

"You're free," he whispered, hoarsely. "But we must go! Now!"

She ran with him now, tightly clutching his hand, down to the edge of the island that faced mainland Ireland. They needed only to cross the thin strait, then run to freedom.

But the tide was still distressingly high. Moreover, a damp patchy fog was settling itself onto the island, obscuring almost everything in sight. It looked as if there were no mainland at all, as if Inis Ghall were the only piece of land in the entire world.

An overturned curragh sat by the edge of the sea. Aedan realized it must be Donnacha's; likely his uncle had dragged it here and left it for him. It was a small, roundish thing, animal skin stretched tight over bent and woven willows, a shallow saucer just big enough for two. Aedan had no idea how to sail such a thing, and hesitated at the water's edge.

But Marra seemed to understand at once. Before Aedan had a chance to think about it, she pushed the vessel into the water, then grabbed his hand.

"Aedan! We go!" she shouted.

They waded into the chilled waters and hoisted themselves into the little boat, which felt like a small, violently rocking bed. Aedan grabbed one of the oars.

Shouts came from the interior of the island.

"Come back here!" came a thunderous order, in Spanish.

His father! Aedan was both stunned and infuriated.

"Go to Hell!" he shouted back, the worst curse he could think of, as he tried to paddle away from the island. But the clumsy vessel spun about and knocked against the boulders at the shore. In desperation, he shoved the oar deep into the sandy bottom and pushed the curragh out deeper into the water. It seemed to work: the vessel caught on a current and seemed to be drifting away from Inis Ghall, just as the fog began to lift somewhat, revealing a group of men heading toward them. Jacobo's shouts were growing louder.

"Don't be a fool! Come back now, and spare yourself!"

The curragh drifted farther into the strait, rocking violently. Marra gripped the bent-willow edge, a panicked look on her face, while Aedan tried to push the little vessel out farther and away. But he could not tell what direction they were heading in; they might well be floating west into the open sea for all he knew.

Suddenly there was a great explosion of sound, a giant clap of thunder and light. Someone was shooting at them, with the hand-cannon! Aedan struggled to make out whom. It was not his father, who was now shouting and gesturing violently, but Murtogh's very own Irish warriors, who had commandeered Jacobo's weapon. And they were not shooting just gunpowder, either. Something hurtled toward them, grazing the edge of the boat, sending it spinning and ultimately, capsizing.

Aedan and Marra were thrown into the water. Aedan felt the shock of the icy ocean enveloping them, the world turning wet, green and gray and ultimately black.

26.

It did not take long for Marra to catch her bearings. Despite the cold, the bleak light and fog, she was at home in the sea and knew how to move in water. But Aedan, it was clear, did not. She watched in fear as he flailed about, and began to sink.

The water in the strait was not very deep. Within hours, the tide would roll out and they would be able to wade through it. But now it was a full foot over their heads and lashed with waves: enough to drown in.

Marra reached toward Aedan and grabbed at his yellow hair, pulling him back to the surface, where he sputtered and gasped for air. The curragh floated helplessly away from them, bobbing on the surface of the water right-side up now. The oars were lost.

They were somewhere between Inis Ghall and the mainland, but they might as well be alone in the middle of the vast western sea. Their sight was obscured by the relentless fog; their world had become nothing but water and seaweed.

With her arm firmly about Aedan's neck, Marra tried to pull him toward the mainland shore. But he was panicking and struggled against her, as people

223

unfamiliar with water will do. Desperately, she tried to pull him along, by his garments, but he was heavier than she, taller; it seemed a hopeless task.

She felt herself sinking with him. As she did so, she had a sudden vision of her home island, the palm trees and flat white sand, turquoise waters. She saw her mother, lovingly combing her hair with a bone comb. Her brothers, alive and handsome. Then she saw their corpses on the beach, as the *Caribe* had left them. She saw herself pearl-fishing with her father, laughing with delight over the size of their catch. The great beast-ship in the eastern horizon; the strange pale men stealing them away from their canoe…her own great escape into these very waters, the jump from the big ship into the black icy sea.

Had she undergone all that, just to die now, stupidly, in a mere seven, eight feet of water? These strange, jumbled visions gave her a new burst of energy and courage, and she yanked Aedan back to the surface of the water with all her strength.

She did not know her captors' word for *swim*. "Aedan! Move arms! Legs. Don't fight with sea." She shut her eyes for a brief moment, invoking her sea god. *Great God Yocahu, God of the seas, help us. Let us live.*

Aedan, barely conscious, felt himself slide into a dreamlike sort of state, where scenes from his former life mingled with the terrifying reality of cold and wet. He saw himself standing on the other side of St. Alban's, its huge iron gate locked shut. He sat in the snug library, poring over charts and maps of the Western sea; he was laughing with Jacobo in a Galway inn; sitting in silent meditation with Lord Fulke. The vicar's thin, ascetic face seemed to float before him, beckoning to him. "Come to me, Aedan, my son. Come home to me now."

No my lord, I cannot. God forgive me, but I cannot join you in Heaven yet.

He saw Marra lying beside him, asleep in the cave by the sea, a hole of deep blue sky above. The sea birds sang their raucous songs outside, careening up and about the cliffs, as if mocking them. They mocked them still. He heard their screams of laughter above, as he flailed and sank, as brine water filled his mouth and lungs.

Dear Almighty Lord, he prayed now, *please do not take us just yet, not when we have just found each other, not as we are just finally escaping into freedom...*

Marra appeared before his eyes: He saw her tawny oval face, her coal-black eyes. Was it a vision, or reality? Her voice was strong in his ears, insistent. *Go with sea,* she was saying: *Don't fight sea.*

Marra *was* there beside him, it wasn't a vision; he could see her now though the blurry water, her claret-colored gown ballooning about her, her black hair waving about her like seaweeds. Gradually, he began to relax and felt himself rising, bobbing in the water. He moved his limbs as Marra did and found he did not sink: He emerged from beneath the waves and the air he sucked in seemed unbearably sweet. He kicked his legs into the fathoms of the ocean, and found himself moving forward, with Marra by his side.

The little curragh suddenly bounced back toward them, actually bumping up against the side of Aedan's head: A rough gift, he thought, from the Almighty. Gasping, he lunged for it and pulled himself into the little limpet-shell boat. Then he reached for Marra.

But as he did so, the thread of the twisted-cotton fiber around his neck snapped at last, and the golden pearl fell into the sea. The precious pearl, born of a humble foreign oyster, the pearl that caused so much joy and pain, covetousness and grief, slipped forever from his grasp. He actually saw it for an instant underwater, the small iridescent orb lazily sinking into the viscous green sea, a distant planet too far from his grasp. He could dive to retrieve the pearl, or snatch Marra into the curragh. He could not do both.

He yanked Marra by the sodden red-wool skirt of her gown and pulled her into the boat, nearly falling back overboard with her in the process. She landed against him with a hearty thud and the little round boat spun and rocked crazily. Gasping for air, laughing and giddy with strange joy, utterly soaked to the bone, they embraced each other tightly inside the vessel. They curled up against each other as they rocked violently in the waves, waiting silently to see where the currents would take them. Eventually, when the sea itself calmed, they drowsed into a light sleep, in the soft light of dawn.

The sun burned behind his eyes. Aedan opened them, and looked up into a brilliant sky of blue, dotted with black and white sea birds. The sea rushed and roared about them, a muted lullaby.

Marra still lay tight beside him in the curragh, which now rocked gently like a baby's cradle. Night and dawn were far behind them, as was Inis Ghall. But where had they ended up? Had they foundered into the vast open ocean of the west? If so, they would surely die.

He struggled to crane his head up and at first, his worst fears seemed confirmed; he saw nothing but the endless sea, layers of frothy waves stretching out to infinity. But then he turned, as a fog-cloud ahead lifted to reveal a cheering vision beyond.

Not Heaven nor Hell. But a thin line of green lay ahead, underneath the welcoming canopy of afternoon sky. Using his arms as oars and paddles, he forced the curragh in the direction of the land ahead.

They came ashore on a deserted beach, a stretch of gravel dotted with boulders and rounded stones, but also the wrecked curraghs of long-ago fishermen. It did not seem much different than the coastline of Inis Ghall. Aedan looked into the tide-pools and saw waving fronds of dulse and carrageen, and the familiar flattish peaks of gray limpets and winkles crowding the stones.

"This is no foreign land," he said, with some relief, "but only another part of Eire." He felt nonetheless as if they had made an ocean journey of epic proportions, and he would not have been surprised to wash up on one of Brendan's isles of forges or ice columns.

"Perhaps we have even reached the mainland, though I cannot quite tell…"

Marra stepped from the boat, her dark hair flying about wildly, along with tattered threads from the hem of her gown. Her face was tense.

"Men? I see none. " She looked about warily. "No men. No beasts."

"There are surely some about. But I don't think we are in O hEynne territory anymore." He yelped out a greeting into the void of gorse and brush and trees and rock. His voice echoed slightly, but there was no response.

They left the battered curragh on the beach, and ventured up around a bend, encountering no other humans or signs of life. Aedan did not know whether to feel relieved about this, or frightened.

They stooped by the shore rocks and ate their fill of limpets. By now Aedan had become used to the fishy chewiness of them, but he had to eat most of a rock-full to fill his empty stomach. From now on, he thought, this is how they would have to live, literally off the sea and earth. There would be no kindly kitchen brother to set plates of steaming food before him at mealtime; no linen-clad pallet to sink into after a long day.

But he had Marra. And they were free.

After they had eaten their fill, they lay on flat rocks overlooking the sea, warming themselves in the sun.

"We have found our own Garden of Eden," he told Marra, with a laugh. "Just you and me on this isle. Why, we are savages!" He laughed again. "Primitive folk, Adam and Eve. " He suddenly jumped up, to survey his new domain. "We've discovered a new land! Our land, our kingdom. You and I shall rule this place and no one else!"

"We free," Marra murmured, scarcely seeming to believe it.

They lay on the sun-warmed rocks for some time, dozing, recovering from their ordeal at sea. Marra curled up against him, nestling her head into his shoulder.

"No more bad," she whispered to him. "Only good."

27.

Twelve years passed...

The fifteenth century rolled into the sixteenth, and the English continued to tighten their grip on the Irish; the sailors of Europe continued their exploration and ventures into the unknown world. Rumors reached Eire of the discovery of new lands to the far West, though they were believed to be the edges of the remote Oriental Spice islands. But this mattered little to the Irish fishermen and clam-diggers and eelers who occupied Eire's western coastline and sea islands, those who continued to live their lives as their ancestors had before them.

A fisherman from a remote Connemarra island which had become known as Inis Bhrendain, or Brendan's Isle, steered his sailed, sturdy wooden vessel down south along the Connemarra coast and into Galway Bay. There, where the bay opened to the sea, he made his way along the northern coastline to a tiny island which lay just off the mainland.

Vicious storms over the years had altered the coastline of Inis Ghall, severing forever its tie to the mainland of Ireland. It seemed to float by itself in the sea now, its great gray cliff still as imposing as ever.

The fisherman Aedan pulled his boat onto the once-familiar western strand, and looked about. It seemed nothing about the island had really changed since he fled here with his wife, so many years ago. He glanced up at the arched caves facing the sea and the seabirds still circling and cawing and crying from above. He smiled, feeling a surge of nostalgia. For so long, he had wanted to return to this place for a visit, but the general busy-ness of life kept him from making the journey: His fishing, running the small *clachan* or settlement of the island he himself had named for Saint Brendan; family life, children, his sons...But once he learned how close Inis Bhrendain was to his native isle—only half a day's journey by boat—he determined to make time to visit, to see what had transpired in his absence.

He made his way across a sheep meadow now empty of sheep, to find a village largely empty of people. It seemed Ghall was turning itself into deserted isle. But he saw a wisp of smoke from the chimney of the church's dwelling, and hopefully knocked on the batten door, before creaking it open slightly.

Here he saw his uncle Comgall's dwelling, looking much as it had back in the day: The oak table, the rough-hewn stone hearth. A fire blazed in that hearth, tended by a tall, fair girl, nearly a woman, who turned a surprised look toward Aedan. And on the straw pallet in the corner—

could that be his own uncle, stretched out like an invalid?

"Are you Itta?" He asked the girl by the fire. "I am your cousin Aedan, come back to visit. Likely you don't remember me—"

"Aedan!" The invalid suddenly rose up from his bed, lifting his arms. "My nephew, the son of Fiona! Praise our benevolent Lord God!"

"Father!" Itta scolded. "You must rest, don't move." Then to Aedan: "He is not deathly ill, it is only the ague he gets in his joints this time of year. Makes him stiff."

"Come here, come here!" Comgall crowed, beckoning to him. "Why, we thought you were long lost, gone. Passed up into Heaven! Yet here you are! How did you ever escape?"

"We landed on a deserted isle, outside the bay, but only half a day's journey from here. I am sorry I could not come back sooner..."

"And the girl, the dark maiden..."

"I remember the dark girl!" said Itta suddenly, a light coming into her eyes. "It must have been very long ago, but I remember my brother painting her. I remember her lovely brown skin, and dark, dark hair."

Aedan smiled. "Marra is my wife and the mother of my three sons. Another child to come, soon."

"That's splendid, boy, splendid. Very different than the life you imagined for yourself at St. Alban's, is it not?"

"I am not unhappy," Aedan said, with a grin. "My boys are dark, like little Mediterraneans. I am deciding now on how best to have them educated. Where is your son, Colm?"

"Ah, he is in France! He studied with your teachers in Galway. Now he is working with a fresco painter there, so he might come back and decorate all the fancy Norman chapels in Galway and Limerick and Dublin."

"I'm happy to hear it. But what has happened to all the people of Inis Ghall?"

"Ah, my boy. They never quite recovered from the fever, or the pirates. One by one, they started to return to the mainland. Then after the Great Storm, which took out our tide-path, they went in a great bunch. There are still a few elderly folks here, a handful to say Mass to on Sunday. But I'm afraid there is not much future on this island."

"You and Itta could come to our island. We could use a priest, we have none. The isle was deserted when Marra and I landed there, twelve years ago. A plague had killed many of the residents, and others fled. It's under the rule of the O Mallaigh, but they ignore it, as the O hEynne ignored this island. Some of the inhabitants have returned, and some fishermen from the north came to settle with us. We have a thriving *clachan* now, it is a good place to live."

"It is something to consider. The O hEynne are no more, we are part of the O Mallaigh territory now, too. But Murtogh's oldest daughter still lives in the tower on the mainland, with the man she married — a Spaniard, from your father's crew!"

Aedan chuckled bitterly. "Ah, my former father, Jacobo. I had not thought of him in a long while. I suppose he is in his dotage on warm Madeira now, still cursing his wayward Irish-born son—"

Comgall gave him a look of surprise. "De Adamo never made it back to Madeira. Ah, but you can't have known that."

"What happened to him?"

"He died, here in Eire. Just after you left, Murtogh and his men seized his ship and crew. They plundered the ship and took it for themselves; and put Jacobo in a gaol on the mainland. He died there, in chains. His crew scattered about, some staying in Connemarra, others escaping to Galway city."

"Indeed," said Aedan softly, considering this turn of events. "So much for his empire of wine and wealth in the Western Sea."

"Well, I suppose as his only son and heir, you might go there and claim his lands and house. You could be quite rich."

"I have no interest in that. I would be curious about the voyage itself, but I have no need for riches and wealth, I have all I need on Inis Bhrendain. My old longing for adventure is sated in my work as a fisherman. I became a fisher of fish, not souls!" He laughed. "It is hard labor, but I have come to love the open sea, unpredictable as it is."

"And your wife? Is she as happy as you are?"

"I believe so. She takes enormous pleasure in our children. She taught them to swim in the ocean, and she tells them stories each night of her old island home, her days as a pearl-fisher." He smiled. "I don't know if the boys quite believe her tales, but we are all entertained by them. And she has become known as something of a healer on our island, she cares for island's sick and brews up all kinds of potions and teas as cures. The other islanders think nothing of her brown skin and dark hair; they consider her as Irish as they are, and she does speak our tongue now, rather well. "

"She has found a place in our world," said Comgall gently. "Could the same be said for any of us, thrown up by chance on her distant isle?"

"I think not," said Aedan, with a grin.

"Will you return, nephew? When you do, we will leave with you, Itta and I. You see she is almost a woman now. I would like her to find a good husband, raise a family —"

"I don't want to marry!" Itta protested.

"Nonetheless," Comgall continued, ignoring her outburst. "I would need some time to prepare my remaining parishioners. Send word to Colm. "

"I understand, uncle. I will try to return in a month's time, would you be ready by then?"

"Yes, yes indeed."

Aedan then walked back across the empty isle, back to the cliffs at the western shoreline where his vessel was beached. He stood for a moment at the base of the cliff, then impulsively began to climb up the rocky face. He climbed to the topmost arch, the cave he had shared that first night he spent with Marra, the place the Basque pirates had dragged him out of. He crouched on the ledge above the sea, and looked inside.

It looked exactly as it had back then, a few black coals sitting in the makeshift hearth, a neat pile of limpet and winkle shells nearby. There was what remained of his fine Galway green-wool cloak, reduced to rotted threads. There was even the big clamshell still sitting by the front entrance, overflowing with rainwater. He entered the cool darkness of the cave, and sat there a moment, listening to the birds. Then he spotted something familiar glinting by the hearth. He picked up it up: It was the pearl-oyster valve Jacobo had given to him years ago in the Galway inn, its interior still glowing iridescent. A shell, from Marra's island. He smiled, pleased to have a special gift to bring back home to his wife.

He then crouched by the entrance of the cave and looked out to sea. The birds cried and screamed, but out in the bay, he saw the outlines of several ships, sails fluttering, as they headed west out of the bay, into open ocean and the great world beyond.

A historical note from the author

In 1492, Christopher Columbus sailed west from Spain and thought he had found the spice islands of the East Indies. He set foot on a small island off the North Atlantic coast--today the Bahamas--populated by a peaceful and friendly tribe of Native Americans known as the Lucayans, a branch of the South American and Caribbean Arawak peoples. My heroine Marra, on the other hand, might have been a Taino, also an Arawak offshoot, and would have come from a Caribbean island a bit further to the south, where precious pearl oysters would be more commonly found.

What prompted Columbus to make this journey in the first place? Some scholars and historians think the idea may have come to him in the year 1477 when he visited Galway in Ireland. At that time, Galway was a flourishing port, a jumping-off place for voyages to the west, in particular Greenland and Iceland; and Columbus did indeed sail to Iceland that same year, and even a little bit beyond.

Columbus saw something in Ireland that profoundly startled him, and may indeed have spurred him to consider sailing west. In the margin of a book he owned, he scribbled an excited note. The following is my own (very loose) translation of the original Latin:

"Strange men have come forth here...We saw washed on the shore of Galway, in Ireland, two bodies with extraordinary features, a man and his wife in a dugout canoe. Surely they came here from Cathay."

Through the years, residents of Western Ireland have reported odd things occasionally washing ashore on their beaches, such as tropical driftwood, foreign seed-pods and even coconut husks. This is not unusual when you consider the Gulf Stream runs from the Caribbean Sea up across the Atlantic and right along Ireland's coast. If not for this ocean current, Ireland's climate might well be as cold as Labrador in Canada, which sits on the same latitude.

The Basques of northern Spain were long known as intrepid sailors and fishermen. They are a brave, honest people, and though my pirates are largely of that nationality, the Basques as a whole are no more or less roguish than any other nationality of Europe. The origin of these people is not known, for their language does not much resemble other European languages. Some historians believe that the Basques, in their tireless search for codfish, whale oil and other riches, traveled far out into the Atlantic (known in medieval times as the Western Sea), perhaps even reaching the coast of Brazil, decades before Columbus even thought to try sailing west. The Vikings, of course, reached the northern tip of Newfoundland in North America even centuries before this. Ancient peoples were far more well traveled than we might ever suspect.

In researching this book, I traveled to Ireland and the places where the book is set, Galway city and locations along the bay and western coast. There is no actual place called Inis Ghall off Ireland's west coast--*gall* means "foreigner" in Irish—but there are hundreds of islands off Connemarra which could be considered similar. My Irish ancestral line descends from the 'Black Irish' family of O hAllmurrain, or Halloran, from County Mayo, but thought to be originally from the Galway area, where in medieval times, they controlled the land the city sits on today before the arrival of the Normans and the English. The name O hAllmurrain means 'foreigner,' and the name is thought to have originated with invading Vikings who stayed behind on the West coast of Ireland, an idea I hope to explore more fully in a series of historical novels dealing with foreigners in Ireland over the years.

I am grateful for all the help I received in researching this book, not only in Ireland, but here at home. In particular, I wish to acknowledge the Seumus MacManus collection of rare Irish books at Seton Hall University's Walsh Library, which proved a true treasure-trove of Celtic history; I'm very grateful to the University Archivist, Prof. Alan Delozier, for his kind help and patience. I also would like to thank the Irish-American Association of Northwest Jersey, where I studied the *Gaeilge*, or Irish language, under a true master, Liam Hart; and the Irish-American Heritage Museum in New York State, which helped in locating some hard-to-find books, including the outstanding *History of Galway* by Seán Spellissy. I am grateful, too, to my own family, many of whom accompanied me to Ireland and provided invaluable support: My parents Michael and Valerie Petersen, my sisters Ginny Roback, Laura Corey and Michaela Petersen, my brothers Matt and Chris Petersen; as well as my own beautiful daughter Francesca Rose and my ever-patient husband Frank, who helped with the design of this book and provided helpful advice, particularly in the area of medieval artillery and hand-cannons!

Go dté tú slán!

2151868R00121

Printed in Great Britain
by Amazon.co.uk, Ltd.,
Marston Gate.